W9-CBZ-094

MAY 0 0 2018

DRIVING BY STARLIGHT

Driving by Starlight

ANAT DERACINE

GODWINBOOKS

HENRY HOLT AND COMPANY · NEW YORK

Henry Holt and Company, *Publishers since 1866*
Henry Holt® is a registered trademark of Macmillan Publishing Group, LLC
175 Fifth Avenue, New York, NY 10010 • fiercereads.com

Copyright © 2018 by Anat Deracine
All rights reserved.

Library of Congress Cataloging-in-Publication Data is available.
ISBN 978-1-250-13342-7

Our books may be purchased in bulk for promotional, educational, or business
use. Please contact your local bookseller or the Macmillan Corporate and
Premium Sales Department at (800) 221-7945 ext. 5442 or by e-mail at
MacmillanSpecialMarkets@macmillan.com.

First edition, 2018 / Designed by Liz Dresner

Printed in the United States of America

10 9 8 7 6 5 4 3 2 1

FOR RASHA, LAMIA, SABA, HUMA,
AND ALL THE GIRLS OF RIYADH

1

INSH'ALLAH

"Do you ever think about leaving?" I asked Mishail, careful to keep my tone casual.

"Lean back, or you'll get shaving cream on the carpet," Mishail said.

"Serves you right for having a carpet in the bathroom," I said, not sure whether I was disappointed or relieved that Mishail hadn't answered my question. I thought about adding a clarification. *I mean, someday. If it were even possible.*

"I can't believe you've never done this before," Mishail said. "Do I have to teach you everything?"

"Yes," I said, hoping she could hear my gratitude.

"You're so ridiculous. Anything involving real life and you're as useless as a six-year-old."

I scowled. I could fix electrical appliances, manage household finances, and carry home bleeding chickens from the butcher, but as far as Mishail was concerned, if you didn't have your own personal style, wear makeup, or dance, you had no practical life skills.

"Just watch what you're doing, or I'll throw you down the stairs."

"You won't hurt me," Mishail said, sounding so smug. I felt a prick of annoyance. Mishail was far too trusting. Last week, when we ditched school to get ice cream, I read the street signs, avoided SUVs that might have been religious police, and navigated crossing the four-lane highway to get to the store across the street. Mishail twirled sunflowers and stopped to pet stray cats, completely oblivious to the men who turned to look at her.

The ice-cream store had the usual sign that all restaurants did when they didn't have a family section—WOMEN AND ANIMALS NOT ALLOWED. Mishail didn't even see it, didn't notice that the guy gave us free ice cream to get us out before any police saw us inside. And on the way back to school, while I plotted excuses in case we were caught, she giggled madly because her mouth was frozen and she was high on sugar. At some point, she laughed so hard she collapsed in a heap, leaving me to practically carry her back.

As if we weren't conspicuous enough, two girls loitering unescorted on the streets of Riyadh in the middle of the day. It was a miracle we hadn't been arrested.

"No, I don't think about leaving," Mishail said, concentrating on the razor's path. "We're not going to get scholarships. No sense in getting our hopes up. Besides, my father won't even let me stay over at your *house*, and yours . . ."

I bit my lip, wondering why I'd asked the question when I knew what the answer would be. Sometimes we fed each other's madness. Sometimes Mishail said, "Sabiha Madam is coming back after her baby, let's surprise her with balloons," and I said, "What if there were so many balloons in the classroom that she had to burst them even to get in?"

But sometimes we had to burst each other's bubbles. Mishail's jaw clenched. I knew she didn't want to finish her sentence.

Say it, I prayed silently. *Say it so I won't have to. Say it, and I won't hope anymore.*

"*Insh'allah*," Mishail said, instead, and my stomach did a somersault. *If God wills.* "Maybe your father will come home by the time we graduate."

"*Insh'allah*," I agreed. "Maybe by then the law will change, and we won't need their permission."

Our eyes met. We'd been doing this for years now, stoking the fires of each other's hopes even though all reasonable people knew there was no way out. The sane thing to do was to keep your head down and do what you were told, so the *muttaween*, the religious police from Al-Hai'a,

3

the Committee for the Propagation of Virtue and Prevention of Vice, wouldn't take away what little freedom you still had.

"The olive dress is going to look incredible on you," Mishail said. "Lift up."

I raised my arms so Mishail could reach my armpits with the razor. Her breath huffed against my face, soft like everything about her. Someday, I promised myself, I'd understand what it was about Mishail that made us love her with the kind of devotion that started and ended wars. Of course she was beautiful, but not in the movie-star way, and that wasn't it at all. Mishail's gift was that her every word felt like a hug. She smiled at strangers with the innocence of never having had to bargain down vendors at the *souq*.

I was different.

"You walk as if you're angry with the world, as if you've got a knife hidden in your shoes," Mishail had said once. My mother had said it differently, and she'd used *that* word, the one that always made me so angry I couldn't even think.

"Everything about you is so . . . *sharp*. Your mind, your voice, your shoulders, even your walk. You remind me so much of your father."

"Stop that," Mishail said, slapping my cheek lightly as I frowned. "Why do you always worry so much? Why can't you just be excited about tomorrow?"

As far as our plots and pranks went, this one was going to be simple, but we were still going to give it everything we had. People who didn't really know Mishail, who saw only the minister's daughter and never the girl, thought she was the most perfectly mannered lady they'd ever met. That it was only my bad influence that got her in trouble.

They don't know, I thought. The girl wolfed down entire *shawarmas* in thirty seconds flat, invented naughty versions of Disney songs, and had lace lingerie smuggled in from an aunt in Paris hidden in the crevice of the air conditioner. The girl could tune out the world for hours only to return to it with the wisdom of a demented Moses, saying calmly, "Before we graduate, we should paint the school wall fuchsia."

Only I knew that Mishail.

A man's voice boomed below us. "HOW MANY TIMES do I have to—"

Mishail flinched, and the razor cut me.

Sorry, Mishail mouthed.

I shook my head. *Not your fault.* The minister had that effect on everyone.

"I'm so sorry," Mishail said. "He gets worse every—"

"Are you sure I won't look stupid?" I asked, deliberately changing the subject. There was one certain way to ruin an evening, and that was letting Mishail talk about her father. "I don't know how to carry myself in a dress, and I feel like a giraffe in heels."

"We'll practice," Mishail said. "If you're not going to care about what you wear, why complain about the *abaya*?"

Mishail had a point. I fought the flutter in my stomach. Sure, it was against school rules to wear anything but the uniform, but that wasn't what was bothering me. Leena Hadi did not wear dresses, had never worn dresses, and wanted to punch the color pink in the face.

A loud knocking at Mishail's bedroom door startled us. Mishail's mother said, "Girls, I want you both down for dinner in five minutes flat."

"It's not fair," Mishail said. "He yells at her, so she yells at us to feel better."

"Don't," I said, toweling off. My legs tingled. "Just think about tomorrow."

Mishail said nothing.

I squeezed her wrists. "Hey, we're not them. Nothing they do can touch us. Remember?"

"We'll have to smuggle the clothes in our schoolbags," Mishail said, relaxing with a sigh. "The park is walled, so there should be no religious police to worry about, only teachers. We'll change in the bathroom and cover up with the *abayas*."

We ate dinner in silence, three women huddled over the table in the kitchen. In the living room, the minister sat with Mishail's brothers. It hadn't always been this way, women in one room, men in the other, sharing dishes by passing them silently through the barely open doorway. All

6

that happened after Mishail's father became part of the government. Before that—

There was no use thinking about the past.

Still, it was better than being at my house, with my mother running around the kitchen trying to cook five dishes at once for a delivery order that was already late, while Fatima Aunty gave apocalyptic sighs and made delicate comments about our "unfortunate situation."

"He's in jail," I said once, shutting her up momentarily. "Just say it. Do you know how many people's fathers are in jail in this country? It's practically normal. Just pack the hummus."

"So, Leena, are you excited about Al-Kharj tomorrow?" Mishail's mother asked.

"Yes, of course," I said. "It's the one day of the year we're allowed to be outside."

"Just be careful," Mrs. Quraysh said. "If you're out in the sun too long, you'll become dark. Don't sit on the grass. And no matter what you do, don't use the bathrooms. That's how you get MERS."

I choked on my laugh. Mishail's toes pinched my calf under the table, but her expression didn't change. How did Mishail stand this day after day? I had to pack my own lunches, but most days Mishail wasn't allowed to brush her own hair. I wondered which was worse.

No wonder she wants to let loose tomorrow, I thought, and my mind returned to the olive dress Mishail had picked out for me. My stomach settled. If it would make Mishail happy, I'd gladly dance around in a clown outfit in front of the headmistress herself.

We settled in beside each other on Mishail's bed. She wasn't allowed over to *my* house, not when there was "no male authority figure to keep the women in check," as the minister put it. But I could stay here, as long as I stayed out of the minister's way. There was never a night that I didn't want to stay in Mishail's coral-toned bedroom, with the magazine clippings of our favorite pop stars hidden under the mattress and Mishail's phone under the pillow playing music until we fell asleep.

The alternative was listening to the soft scratching of cockroaches and the clipped, drip-drip sounds of my mother's sobs through the wall. Once, I tried to comfort her, but she just screamed at me to go away. I understood. The last thing I wanted was anyone seeing how miserable I really was, either.

Mishail curled into my outstretched arm with a contented sigh, and I pushed the bangs out of her face. There was a saying that the strength of an Arab woman was that she slept through the scorpion's sting so her husband's rest was undisturbed. If my nightmares ever woke Mishail, she never let me know. And she never complained.

I fell asleep slowly, wondering if I'd have another of the dreams where I could fly.

The dreams weren't complicated. They always began

the same way, with my sneaking out of the school auditorium while everyone else was at an assembly, and stepping out onto the football field, where we weren't allowed to play because it was obscene for women to jump around. I'd start sprinting so fast that my feet would leave the ground, the folds of my black *abaya* no longer getting between my legs but spreading out like falcon wings. I'd fly over the ten-foot-tall school wall, past Al-Hai'a buzzing around in their tinted vans, and headed straight for Riyadh's Kingdom Tower. The dreams had gone on so long that the ups and downs of flying were now as familiar as the buoyancy of an elevator.

This high up, the pincers of the tower and the sky-bridge that connected them were lit, crackling and alive with electricity. All I had to do was go through, thread the needle, and I'd be free. Just then, I'd see Mishail's face, gazing up at me from below or reflected in a window, and I would plummet to the ground. I'd wake up with a gasp from the fall, heart racing until I saw Mishail fast asleep by my side.

Leaving meant leaving Mishail. It was never going to happen.

2

HARAAM

Al-Kharj! Even the name was as crisp as the city's lush orange orchards. The leaf-green minarets along the road were such a change from the flat red plateau of Riyadh. I ached to open the windows, but the train of school buses heading down the highway had dark contact paper on the locked windows so nobody could see the girls inside.

A white pickup truck rolled up beside our bus, young immigrant boys standing up on the flatbed to feel the breeze. They craned their necks to see us.

"So desperate! I think they're looking for Mishail!"

"Who *isn't* looking for Mishail? Look at how red she's become."

The boys wore tight jeans instead of the white *thobes* Saudi men were expected to wear. *Modern guys*, I thought with envy. My jealousy only increased when the boys turned up the radio and started dancing to a remix of Michael Jackson's "Billie Jean" with Ya Khadija. Their bright, checkered headscarves fluttered against their tasseled leather jackets.

"In September or in June, boys must have their jackets," Mishail said, hiding her face in my headscarf.

"Let them roast! Don't we have to burn in our *abayas*?" I said.

"You talk as if you don't think they look good in them," Mishail whispered to me. I blushed, and Mishail laughed softly against my burning ear.

"Shouldn't they be wearing seat belts?" Aisha asked, ever the practical one.

"Seat belts? First, they need to sit inside the car, and they're too cool to stop dancing," I said as harshly as I could so the other girls wouldn't think I liked boys. I knew that behind my back they sometimes called me *Leena Adhaleena*, which meant *Leena who goes astray*. But there was a big difference between breaking school rules and breaking the law. Colored clothes could get you sent to the headmistress's office. Boys got you beheaded.

I grinned at Aisha, who, along with Sofia and Bilquis, was part of today's conspiracy. I had drawn them maps from my memory of last year's trip. The maps marked the location of the bathrooms, the clearing where the teachers would collect for a break, and the uncharted area behind the hill, which would be our party location.

"It's just that it's our last year together," Mishail had said last week, her gaze low, as if she were confessing to a terminal illness. "I'm sick of the same old class photos. All of us in three rows, standing-sitting-kneeling, hands to our sides as if we're in the army, nothing but our eyes showing from a mountain of black *abayas*. That's just not us, is it?"

Mishail was brilliant. Ask the girls to break a stupid rule for their own fun, and they'd turn into religious nuts in five seconds flat. But cry to them about love and friendship and our last time together, and they'd follow in a heartbeat.

Aisha, Miss Practical, had, of course, been concerned about all the details. How were we going to coordinate, when would we do the switch, what was the signal, how were we going to get any photos taken? Aisha's anxiety was a new development. She used to show up to school wearing nothing but underwear under her *abaya* when the days got too hot for the full-sleeved, ankle-length uniform. Sabiha Madam had suspected something and asked her to take it off. I came to Aisha's rescue, saying, "But, ma'am, isn't it *haraam* to ask a woman to take off her *abaya* if she doesn't want to?"

Now Aisha cared about the details. Thankfully, she hadn't fully converted to being a good girl, and she owed me, at least a little. But she had a point about the photos.

Even if it wasn't *haraam*, all women's cell phone cameras were smashed at the time of purchase. When it didn't make my blood boil, I thought it hilarious that the white-bearded *imams* of the Permanent Committee for Religious Research were so scandalized by the possibility of women taking indecent duck-faced selfies that they found the need to issue a *fatwa* against it. Mishail and I had even made up a song about it. These days, one of us had only to hum the tune to set the other one off in a fit of giggles.

> Everything is *haraam*,
> Don't believe me, ask the *imam*.
> Wearing perfume, not wearing perfume
> Boys and makeup will take us to hell,
> Skirts and swimsuits and TV as well.
> Everything is wrong,
> Even singing this song.

"I have a pocket camera," Mishail had said. "My brother got it from duty-free this summer. It's small enough that they'll never find it on me. We'll post the photos to a private account."

"You promise it'll be private?" Aisha asked.

"We promise," I said, looking at Mishail for confirmation; we'd been speaking in the first person plural for as long as I could remember. "This is just for us, not for outsiders."

"Will we be taking off our *hijab*?" Bilquis asked. "I mean, colored clothes are one thing, but showing your hair is serious."

"Actually, the idea of *hijab* never appears anywhere in the Quran," I said. "The *jilbab* does appear in the Hadith, but even then—"

"Oh, shut up already, Leena Lawyer," Sofia said. "We're not your freedom fighters. We'll do whatever we feel comfortable doing, okay? Stop showing off."

"I wasn't!" I said, embarrassed.

"That's all we want anyway, to be ourselves," Mishail said, making peace.

The school buses pulled into the walled orchard of Al-Kharj. We got down fully veiled, and then the bus drivers and male staff left the park. The headmistress shut the gates, and with a glorious roar, all five hundred of us threw off our *abayas* and started running to explore. We seniors headed for the best clearing, the one by the water fountain on which other seniors had been etching their initials since even before we were born. Aisha, Bilquis, Mishail, and Sofia waited quietly on a picnic blanket until our supervising teacher started nodding off. Then I climbed the nearest tree to ensure the coast was clear.

"Head for the walls," I whispered to the others when I got down. "Walk along the boundary until you see the bathrooms to your right. We'll change there. Don't all leave at once."

They spread apart, leaving the rest of the class behind.

I felt a small flutter of anxiety, but Mishail was probably right that these three could be trusted not to melt under the pressure. They'd proved themselves when they wore colored socks to school on Valentine's Day.

All five of us made it to the bathroom without incident, although Bilquis was panting as if she'd been in a fight. We changed in the stalls, squealing, giggling, daring the others to come out first.

Mishail and I shared a stall; she rolled her eyes at their hysterics. I was too nervous in my dress to respond.

"One second," Mishail said, and adjusted the shoulder strap. "Okay, let's go."

I stepped out, and everyone fell silent. Blood rushed to my ears. Just when I was about to run back into the stall and cancel all the plans, Sofia whistled in her frank way and said, *"Mash'allah*, you have nice legs."

Mishail's eyes said, *I told you.*

"Once we're out of this bathroom, we'll need to run," I said.

"Run?" Bilquis said. "You didn't say that before. I can't run."

I ground my teeth. Girls were always such fools the first time they tried something rebellious. As if they thought all there was to it was having the idea, and they'd be transported daintily through their magical fantasy without being caught.

"At least it's not like when we had to climb out of my

window using the rope ladder," Mishail said. "Remember that?"

"Or when we had to tie plastic bags on our feet because the storm drains were clogged," I said. "Look, guys, things don't always work out as planned. We just have to adapt."

"You're both crazy," Bilquis said, pulling her large, baggy skirt in all directions, as if trying to find something in its folds. "I don't think this is a good idea."

"Come with us or don't," I said. "It's entirely your choice. But we can't stay here where anyone can find us."

Bilquis swayed in the entrance of the bathroom while Mishail, Aisha, Sofia, and I dashed to the walls, hiding behind trees when we could. I felt something tickling my legs and shivered, realizing it was the first time since I was a child that my skin had been exposed to the air. Goose bumps appeared where the soft olive dress rested against my thigh, so I pulled the dress down awkwardly.

Aisha appeared at the tree immediately to my right, wearing what appeared to be an extra-large T-shirt over skinny jeans. A wide belt cinched the T-shirt in at her waist. The four of us arrived at the clearing without any other issues. "Even if nothing else happens, we did this!" Sofia said, throwing her hands in the air. She had on a sleeveless hot-pink blouse with a deep V-neck, and I felt simultaneously embarrassed and envious. My breasts were tiny, so small that I could still get away with passing as a boy. It was convenient to run errands, but that didn't mean I didn't want Sofia's or Mishail's curves.

Mishail pulled out the camera. Without warning, she started singing. Mishail had never been allowed to practice her singing except to recite the Quran, but her voice was so delicate, like the sound of the first rain, that we squealed and clutched one another and started dancing. We were so wild with joy.

Just then, Bilquis appeared.

She was wearing her regular uniform, which should probably have prepared me for the scornful way she laughed and said, "*Wallah*, Leena, prancing like a frightened horse isn't the same thing as dancing."

I turned to her in fury.

"Ignore her," Sofia said, grabbing my arm. "Miss Too Fat to Run is hardly the authority to comment on your dancing skills."

"You girls think way too much of yourselves," Bilquis said. "This is *haraam*, and I'm going to tell the headmistress before it gets out of control."

And she stalked off.

Mishail gasped. It yanked me into action.

"Everyone, get changed," I said. "We can't wait to get back to the bathrooms. When you're done, hand over your clothes. No sense in all of us getting in trouble."

There was no time to waste. I quickly shimmied out of my dress and into my uniform.

"*Now*," I said when the other girls hesitated. "The faster you do it, the less chance anyone will see you. Mishy, give me the camera."

I took Aisha's T-shirt and nodded in approval as she pulled the drawstring of her uniform skirt around the skinny jeans. For the first time, I felt glad of the baggy, unflattering robes that were our uniform. So much could be hidden under them.

"Run," Mishail said. "And no matter what, don't tell anyone anything."

Aisha and Sofia took off immediately, and Mishail gave me an expectant look.

"Never," I said. I held out my hand until Mishail dropped the camera into it. I put it in my underwear.

Mishail's grin was blinding.

We walked back together to the rest of our classmates. The other girls gave us looks that were part fear and part envy, telling me that Bilquis had spread the story beyond just the headmistress. So everyone knew.

Bilquis came to the clearing, looking annoyed instead of triumphant.

"She said she'll deal with you when we're back in school," she said loudly. "Not here."

Mishail sagged in relief.

"If I were you, I'd be nervous," Bilquis said. "She looked really angry."

"If I were *you*, I'd start learning how to run," I said.

Nervous titters ripped through the clearing. I pulled Mishail in for a hug. Aisha and Sofia joined us, as did a few others who were no longer worried about showing whose side they were on.

"Hey, Leena," Mishail said.

"Hm?"

"Don't sit on the grass."

I burst into laughter.

A couple of hours later, when the buses were back at the school, the four of us were escorted to the headmistress's office. I put my palms on my thighs, little finger slightly apart from the rest. The others watched it carefully, as I'd instructed them.

One, I thought, hoping telepathy was real and the others could hear me. *We're in Phase One.*

The key to handling Maryam Madam was recognizing the phases of her anger and waiting them out quietly. Mishail was so attuned to it now that she could keep her head down in perfect ladylike surrender while picking up clues just from the headmistress's voice.

That was anger in the headmistress's tone now, of course, but with the spice of outrage that always accompanied the discovery phase. It was as if Maryam Madam believed that anyone who broke the rules had some deep ulterior motive. When we were caught for the Valentine's Day incident, it was ten minutes of *But WHY SOCKS? What were you REALLY after?* until we entered Phase Two.

"Mishail, what would your father say? What if a man had seen? Why do you girls take such stupid risks for no reason?"

Mishail's ring finger unfolded from her clenched fist. I did the same thing, indicating that we'd entered the second phase: questions. This, too, required no response. Maryam Madam would eventually arrive at the explanation that she liked the most and express her complete disappointment as she entered Phase Three.

"I'm *so* disappointed in you girls. You should be ashamed of yourselves. What kind of role models are you to the young women of our country? Is this worth risking your reputation? Your future? I should make you stand in your underwear so the other girls can point and laugh."

Mishail's head rose almost imperceptibly. Phase Four was creative punishment, and it signaled the end of the cycle. It was only at this juncture that speaking was of any use. I tried to mimic Mishail's look of deep penitence. I probably just looked as if I were in pain.

"We're sorry, ma'am," I said. "We weren't thinking."

"Sorry? I'll show you sorry. Whose idea was this anyway?"

I never understood why the headmistress always asked questions that were impossible to answer. Searching for the origin of our ideas was like trying to pull apart salt and water. It was always one of us saying something and the other saying *yes, yes and also* until even learning to ride a bicycle involved climbing out a window on a rope, and then using it to tie ourselves to one another so one could pull the other along with Rollerblades.

"Last chance. One of you could get punished, or all of you can. So who was it?"

"Me," we said together, and then dropped our heads immediately to hide our grins.

Maryam Madam pinched her temples. I took advantage of the headmistress's closed eyes to mouth *It'll be okay* to the others. All said and done, Maryam Madam was not so bad. She was practical, and if you listened carefully, she always seemed less annoyed at someone's having broken the rules than at their getting caught. It was all, *what if the police* and *think of your parents* and never anything as preachy as Rehmat Madam's "A woman without a *hijab* is like a chair with two legs" or the slogan of Al-Hai'a—*A modest woman needs no mirror.*

"I'm going to get nothing out of you while you're all together," the headmistress said. "You three, go back to class and remain standing for what's left of the day. I need to talk to Leena alone."

3

TUFSHAN

The headmistress opened her mouth to continue, but I shook my head, glancing at the shadows moving below the door. Maryam Madam's eyes rolled upward, as if praying for patience.

"Girls, I know you're listening on the other side."

The shadows cleared, but I waited for the footsteps to disappear down the hallway before I reached into my underwear and pulled out the camera. The headmistress drew in a sharp breath.

"You know how dangerous that is, right? If a photo of the minister's daughter were to get spread around the Internet—I mean, don't you remember the death threats against Princess Basmah when she was caught without her *hijab*?"

"That was different! She was *smoking*. This was just—"

I trailed off at the headmistress's skeptical look. I really didn't know what it was that drove me and Mishail to do these mad, dangerous things. Mostly Mishail, but I had to admit it set my blood on fire, too. Maybe it was something of that *tufshan* my father used to speak of, the strange restlessness that happened to boys from poor families with no *wasta*, no political connections with which to secure their future. At night they could be heard drifting in stolen cars on Dromedary Lane.

Hormones, my mother had said when I asked what *tufshan* meant.

Don't lie to her, my father had said. *Tufsh is the way a man moves when he's drowning. Stuck between fighting and giving up.*

I knew the feeling well now. It wasn't only boys who knew they had been cheated so the thousand grandchildren of this country's founder would never have to work a day in their lives. If *tufshan* drove them to vandalism and crime, to us girls, who could not even do those things, it just drove us mad.

I tried to read Maryam Madam's thoughts. Her silver-streaked hair was tucked neatly into a ponytail. The corners of her eyes were wrinkled and kind. She looked exactly as she had when I saw her for the first time, back in the sixth grade, when she was just a mathematics teacher, the newest member of the school staff.

I would never forget that day. We had been planning how to make sure the new teacher saw things our way.

Too often new teachers came in wanting to prove that they could handle the job and screamed themselves hoarse over stupid things like heart-shaped pendants or earphones under the headscarf, starting a war that ended only when we used the ultimate weapon. We mixed red food coloring with Vaseline and dabbed the teacher's black chair with it to stain her backside when she sat down. It meant public humiliation, threats, tears, and a new teacher, which wasn't actually good for anybody. So we were thinking of something smaller, just to show her where the line was.

But the minute Maryam Madam walked into the classroom, it fell silent, not because she'd screamed "Shut up!" or "Pin-drop silence!" as other teachers had done, but because she had a way of drawing everyone's eyes to her, and making all of us want to hear what she had to say. She held a giant protractor, with chalk attached at one end, and wielded it as if it were a sword. She got straight to the lesson, and when I ignored her to play tic-tac-toe with Mishail, she whirled around and threw a piece of chalk that landed between my eyes like a bullet.

"You think I don't see you," Maryam Madam said. There was no anger in her voice, just crinkled-eye amusement that was more effective than any whip. "But I know who you are, Leena Hadi. And I know you're used to having your way around here. I can see you trying to control the class from that corner of the room. You think that because this stuff comes easy for you, you are some kind of VIP? Why don't you come up here and solve this, then, if you think you can?"

The class had laughed, taking her side. So I stood, held my head up, and solved the problem aloud, adding that because we had an old edition, the answer at the back of the textbook was wrong. I was expecting Maryam Madam to get angry. Instead, her eyes sparkled, and she clapped as if she'd been given the birthday present she'd most wanted. She also seemed to recognize my father on parent-teacher night, because her face lit up at the words *Hadi Mutazil* as if that name meant something to her. They debated politics for an entire hour while other people's parents stood off to the side and whispered about it.

"A remarkable woman," my father had said afterward, as if he couldn't feel the rage my mother was pouring out underneath her *abaya*. "It's a pity about her husband, but I can't imagine it's anything but a relief. Especially since she's now financially independent."

After the arrest, when I spent my days staring out the window to avoid Mishail's concerned glances, and my evenings walking around the streets to avoid my mother's shell-shocked face, it was the headmistress who kept me from the edge of that final cliff. Those rough, chalk-covered hands slapped me, dragged me out of the bathroom by my ears, bandaged my bleeding forearms, and then slapped me again.

"We're on the same side, Leena," Maryam Madam had said, rubbing her eyes tiredly. "I promised your father I'd take care of you, but I can't do it if you're going to set the world on fire. You think I want to be the enemy here? You think I'd do this if I didn't love you? I want what's best for you, and that means making sure you survive your own incredible stupidity."

The words she used were so close to those horrible ones from Rowdha Yousef that were ruining my life—*My Guardian knows what's best for me*—but they felt so different coming from the headmistress. In those days, after the unrest of the Arab Spring, Rowdha petitioned the country's *Majlis* to keep the rules in place that prevented women from acting without the support of their male guardians. Rowdha believed women shouldn't be allowed to drive or even go to the roadside *bakhala* to buy their own maxi-pads, because if women could take care of themselves, men would stop being respectful. Might even leave.

As if my father had chosen to be dragged away from his family by the *mahabith*, leaving us so paralyzed.

"What do you want to do?" the headmistress asked now, interrupting my memory.

"I'd like to print out a few copies," I said. "And then you can delete the digital photos."

"I'll give you some time while I lecture the others."

The headmistress got up and headed out, locking me in for safety. I plugged the camera into her computer. The photos came up immediately, and I blushed. Mishail was a talented photographer, but it was really strange and uncomfortable to see photos of ourselves like this. Sofia's chest glowed with sweat, as if she were a beach model. Aisha's photo was probably the most innocent. She looked irritable and hot. One photo caught me entirely by surprise. I was sitting on the grass, looking directly at Mishail, hands clenched at my sides as if gearing up for a fight. I wondered what had been going through my mind that I would look at Mishail with such intense anger. As if the universe were marking out the contrast, the next photo was of Mishail, whose gentleness and light eyes made her seem almost like a fairy painted into a field of flowers than a real girl.

These photos had no business being online, where anyone could get to them. We would each get a keepsake printout, and that would have to be enough. Sometimes it was as if Mishail forgot that her father was the minister of the interior, whose department owned Al-Hai'a as well as Saudi Telecom. They spied on all phone and Internet communications in the country. Not only did all our phones have apps that regularly pinged our guardians with our location, our fathers could always request the records to determine if there had been any inappropriate communications. Mishail *knew* this, so it was almost as if she were asking to be caught.

I was about to get up when I saw the headmistress's

e-mail pop up with a new message. I read the subject line by accident, and then froze in the chair.

I knew I had no business reading the headmistress's e-mail. I shouldn't even have registered that subject line, though I'd read it on autopilot. But it said *Majlis internship—Deadline for applications Wednesday, October 8*.

That was two weeks from today. I had heard about the program, of course. Now that women could finally vote and even be elected to the council, joining the *Majlis* was the dream of any girl interested in changing the law. Why hadn't the headmistress mentioned it before?

See, if you were a woman in Saudi Arabia, you dreamed of only three things. To marry a man you loved. To change Saudi Arabia. And to leave Saudi Arabia, at least for a little while. As for leaving, there were only two ways out—a KASP scholarship to a foreign university, which required a guardian's permission and more influential connections than I had, or being sold into marriage to the highest bidder, also with a guardian's permission.

So I didn't dream of leaving. And I didn't dream of love. But I did hope that one day I could change things, make our lives more bearable.

There was a sound in the hallway. Footsteps. The headmistress was on her way back. My finger hovered over the message. I had to know. If there was a way, even if it was just the glimmer of light underneath a locked door, I had to know.

I scanned the message swiftly, feeling the skin on the back of my neck prickle. My stomach felt both heavy and cold, as if I'd swallowed a block of ice.

Each school had to submit the names of two participants, who would debate the *sharia* law in a national competition. The winning team would receive full tuition and room and board at Princess Nora University and spend their summers working at the *Majlis*. The winning school would receive a grant that had so many zeros my eyes glazed over.

I marked the message as unread and pulled the photos back up to cover the screen. I went to the printer to hide my face as the headmistress returned. I didn't have Mishail's ability to completely mask my thoughts.

"They kept their mouths shut," Maryam Madam said. "I pretty much had to ask point-blank, *Did any of you bring a camera?* And even then, only Bilquis said anything."

The headmistress glanced at the colored printouts.

"Why do you children have a death wish?" she muttered, sitting at her desk. "Do you have any idea what the minister would do if he knew what the girls at his daughter's school were up to?"

I caught the headmistress's eye. There was no anger there, just exhaustion.

"You take great care of her," Maryam Madam said. "Better than any sister. I've deleted the photos. Here." She handed back the camera. "You did the right thing telling me, Leena."

I frowned in confusion, and then realized I must look conflicted. I was, but not about this. Protecting Mishail came first, no question. The last five years had taught me that to survive, you had to work with the authorities, not against them, bear the scorpion sting if you had to, and I was going to make absolutely sure Mishail survived.

"God forbid any of you start messing around with boys," the headmistress said with a laugh. "This stuff, I can protect you from. If I ever find out any of you girls have betrayed my trust, have gone *there* . . ." She shook her head.

"We'll save that for when we're in university," I said, trying to jokingly guide the conversation back to where I wanted it. "I was thinking Princess Nora for law? Unless you have some other guidance?"

The headmistress fell silent. Her pensive face made me nervous. If I was being considered for the internship, wouldn't Maryam Madam be more excited?

"It'll be tough with your situation," the headmistress said, and my knees trembled. "Even if you're accepted into a university, you need his permission to go. I'll see what I can do. No promises."

I swallowed, trying not to let my disappointment show. I should've expected it. It didn't matter that I was at the top of my class. Merit didn't matter, not in this country. All that mattered was that my father had disobeyed the government, protested against it, and so I would be punished for his sins.

I didn't want to ask any more questions, didn't want to think about what I would do with my life if I wasn't even allowed to study after high school.

The bell rang, signaling the end of the school day.

"Thank you," I said, and walked out. I had no memory of walking back to class. I didn't realize I was clutching the photos so hard I was leaving creases. Most of the girls were hurrying out to the school buses, but Aisha and Mishail were waiting in a corner.

"How'd you manage to do that?" Aisha said. "When Bilquis told her about the camera, we were sure you were in for a full strip search. We were expecting you to come back traumatized."

"I knew she would find out about the camera," I said. My voice felt dull and distant, as if I were reciting from a script. "While she was talking to you, I printed out the photos and hid the pages. She deleted everything from the camera, but printouts are better than nothing, right?"

A weight descended on my shoulders.

If I hadn't said anything, we'd have digital photos that would make us giddy with joy but could ruin our lives at any minute.

If I hadn't said anything, I could have had one more day hoping for a future that I knew now would never be mine.

"You're such a genius," Mishail said, swooping in for a hug. I lifted her off her feet and swept her in a circle, burying my face in her neck and exhaling a hot, heavy breath there. *Worth it*, I told myself. *Just for this moment, it was all worth it.*

4

BOYAT

When I walked with my mother on the street like this, I thought we must look like husband and wife to everyone else. Just another man and woman, nothing to see.

In the simple white *thobe* that all Saudi men wore, I was tall and thin, a sharp contrast to my mother, whose curves weren't concealed even by the shapeless black *abaya*. The checkered scarf and *ghutra* covered my hair, and I'd learned a few tricks over the last few years that made the disguise really work. Other girls had tried this, of course. So many that there was even a word for it: *boyat*. And men desperate for female contact had tried hiding in a black *abaya* and a face-covering *niqab* to get into the Ladies Kingdom at

Mamlaka mall or the women-only zones of Riyadh. But the security guards always caught them, just as the *muttaween* of Al-Hai'a usually caught the *boyat*.

But those women hadn't had to do this practically every day for years. It had usually been a one-time thing, a protest against the rules or an escapade. When it became a daily necessity, you learned quickly not to make mistakes.

I knew how to stand up straight, keeping my shoulders wide to take up more space. Hands had to be kept in pockets, not awkwardly squirming as if hunting for a phantom purse. The real challenge was in what you did with your eyes. Women were used to averting their gaze from other people and the surveillance cameras on the street corners, heads bent toward the ground. Men looked directly at other men, and if you were shifty, nervous, or didn't meet people's eyes, you were not *murwa*, not a man at all.

I had now spent years perfecting the Arab handshake. One long clasp, none of the sweaty firmness with which young, hairless boys tried to prove their manhood, none of the cold and brisk formality with which foreigners were greeted. This was a slow pull, a dance that took you cheek to rough cheek with another man for three quickly exchanged kisses. The first time I did it, with the grocery clerk, I felt dirty and terrified, and I cried all night. It was the first time I'd been touched by a non-*mahram* man, and I was convinced I had polluted my body in the eyes of God.

Maybe the grocery clerk had seen through the disguise the minute his lips touched my hairless cheeks.

All this drama just to run errands.

It was no wonder Mishail loved the challenge of undoing all that training to make me look girlie.

"Did you like it?" Mishail had wanted to know. "When he kissed you. Is he good-looking? Your first real kiss should be with someone good-looking, or it doesn't count."

At the thought of Mishail, I smiled, and the black cloud that had followed me since I found out about the internships cleared a little. Mishail was right. Our future was here, not in dreamed-up adventures we could never have. True, my entire world consisted of my mother and Mishail, and the two of them were spinning away from me with widening and haphazard orbits, as if without my father there wasn't enough gravity to hold our solar system together.

But it was still more than others had, so I told myself to be grateful.

Except that my mother was pinching my elbow.

"Hurry up."

I sped up, remembering that since it was traditional for women to walk a step behind men, when you were the "man," you couldn't get distracted by your thoughts and slow down to a leisurely stroll. Especially if the woman in question needed to get things done.

We stopped at the butcher first, and I played the

tiresome game of telephone between my mother and the supertraditional butcher, who thought that speaking directly to a woman would send him straight to hell.

"She says it's sickly. He says it's just athletic. She says that a healthy chicken should have a—what?"

Another pinch. A signal to move in closer to hear the whispered, "Don't tell him this, because you shouldn't be talking to a man about body parts. But a healthy chicken, or horse, or any other animal, should have large buttocks. The hind legs of this chicken are too small. Not enough exercise."

I sighed and pushed past the butcher, ignoring the indignant squawks from my mother and the sickly chicken, and searched the cages for a chicken with a fat behind.

"That one," I said, and the butcher yanked it out and held it up for inspection. When my mother nodded, I stepped aside so the butcher could weigh it while alive. He held it by its wings and turned it upside down. Too surprised to put up a fight, the chicken fell silent as the butcher slit its throat and allowed the blood to drain.

"Next?" I asked, pretending that carrying the plastic bag full of dead chicken and blood didn't bother me at all.

"Hossein. You remember the house?"

I frowned. There was something odd about the way my mother had mentioned my father's partner in their law practice. Nervous, as if the last time we'd seen Hossein hadn't been just last month.

"What do we need there?"

"I just need some papers signed. None of your business. Do you remember it or not?"

"Of course," I said, "but it's a thirty-minute walk."

We headed there in silence until my mother said quietly, "I can't set up a bank account without your father's permission. I have to write a letter."

I nodded, teeth clenched. I had a hundred questions—*What have we been doing for money so far? Where do you put the money from your catering business? Why do you want a separate bank account? Does that mean he's never coming home?*—but I didn't dare ask any of them.

I kicked the pebbles as we made our way out of the busy marketplace and into the residential area of Suleimaniya. Here, spacious white villas ornamented with bougainvillea alternated with ramshackle redbrick buildings with forbidding metal doors. The houses of Riyadh were usually, as the name said, *riads*, vast and ornate marble and mosaic, all windows facing the interior atrium, no windows facing the outside world. Which meant thousands of narrow, dirty alleyways filled with cats, cockroaches, green Dumpsters, and black garbage bags, but these might lead to large mansions concealed entirely from the outside world.

Like the women, hiding a kilo of gold jewelry and Prada heels under their abayas, I thought, eyeing my mother in her opaque black silks. *Full of secrets.*

"How do you do it, anyway?" my mother asked, breaking the silence. "Remember the way. Your father could do it, but I would get lost in my mother's house."

"I remember landmarks," I said, hoping I wouldn't have to explain further. I didn't want to share my memories. *That's the toy shop where he taught me how to change a battery. This road with slightly fewer potholes is where he taught me how to ride a bicycle. That's where we stopped to see the gray cat eat one of its kittens after giving birth.*

We arrived at the villa. It looked just like all the others, but I knew the one brick that was not like its neighbors. Hossein's son, Faraz, and I had once found a drill and decided to make a peephole at eye level to shoot enemies from. The replacement was smooth, painted wood, not brick, and I felt for it with my fingers.

I rang the bell before my mother could annoy me by asking if I was sure.

Faraz opened the door, and I felt another pinch at my elbow that meant, *Watch how you act around him.* My mother seemed to be under the popular impression that men, and boys in particular, were basically animals, unable to control themselves around women.

"I just don't want him getting any ideas," she'd said once. "You never know. And we have enough problems."

Faraz wasn't related to us, and so he wasn't *mahram* in the strict sense. But we'd grown up together since we were in diapers, and after years of pillow fights and video games and shared lessons in law from his father, how was I going to see him as anything other than a brother?

"*Salaam aleikum*," I said. "So can we come in or not? My mother has some work with your father."

"Sorry, come in. He's on the phone. Will you sit down?"

I watched Faraz carefully as he brought us tea. Mishail was always teasing me about him. Our families were from compatible tribes, so a marriage wouldn't be illegal. Faraz knew about our situation. He wasn't so rich that he could afford to marry anybody he liked. He wasn't at the top of his class, but he wasn't an idiot, either. But he was so young-looking, his cartoon eyes turning into pitying, soupy puddles any time he saw me. I also hated his beard. Mishail was delusional. Just because Faraz was the only boy I'd ever met, it didn't mean I was going to marry him.

We sat quietly. In the background, the television played *Fatullah's Facts*. Imam Fatullah jumped out from behind a green velvet curtain, clapped his hands together, and tossed his long, curly brown hair. Fatullah was the latest in a long line of self-proclaimed "hip" *imams* who had been caught for a street crime and then got out of jail quickly by turning into an *imam* as a demonstration of his commitment to Islam. The trend started with Abu Zekem, who stole and raced cars before being arrested and converting into a *muttawa*, helping the police arrest his former friends.

"*Bismillah-ur-Rahman-ur-Rahim*, and welcome, my young Muslims," Fatullah said. "We have prepared a *tremendous* show for you today, addressing the matters of *aqeedah* that weigh most heavily on your mind. Now, let me begin by reminding you that I am but His humble servant, and I do not offer my own opinions, despite what my opponents say. All truth comes from the *usul al-fiqh*, the Quran, the Hadith, and the *ijma*, and *that*, my friends, is one of—"

"FATULLAH'S FACTS!" chorused the audience, breaking into loud applause. I rolled my eyes.

"Is there nothing else on?" my mother asked Faraz, sounding pained. Faraz switched to the grainy, illegal foreign channels and settled on Al Jazeera. The host was discussing an incident at KAUST. The prestigious university, the only coed one in the country, was temporarily closed, and students were protesting the closure while the *imams* and *muttaween* were celebrating their victory.

"It looks like things are heating up," Faraz said. "The tension can't—"

"Change the channel," my mother said, an edge to her voice. Faraz flinched but obeyed immediately. I tried to apologize with my eyes. My mother had no further patience for the protesters and their revolution. Between her paranoia about government surveillance (which wasn't really paranoia when your husband had been arrested for seditious activity) and her determination to avoid any reminders of the past, she rarely interacted with other people at all. Sometimes I thought she had forgotten how normal women behaved.

Speaking of "normal women," some of those were on *Fatullah's Facts*, asking the host questions from behind a mesh screen.

"Is it permissible to shape the eyebrows?"

"Is it *haraam* to name a baby Rahim?"

"If you dye your hair on earth, will your hair be dyed in paradise?"

"Is it still backbiting if we are warning our brothers and sisters about a person whose mistakes are known to all?"

But there wasn't even the hint of a smile on Imam Fatullah's face. He took every one of these stupid questions seriously, the camera zooming in on his perfect bronze skin and those big eyes with their ridiculously long eyelashes.

"*Walaikum assalam wa rahmatullah*," Imam Fatullah said gravely, and then answered, "Remember what the prophet—peace be upon him—said of slander, that it is saying of another person that which he would not like. Even if what you say is true, you will be following in the footsteps of those hypocrites of Medina who slandered Aisha and were burned with hellfire and given only hot pus to drink as relief."

Applause! What wisdom! What eloquence! I dug my nails into my thigh. How was it fair that a guy like this ended up on TV, rich and famous, with hordes of fools following his "legal" advice, while my father was still rotting away in jail?

Just then, Hossein appeared with his wife. My mother

41

stood, said, "Don't touch anything, don't say anything," and followed the couple into an office.

"No, I don't know why we're here," I said to Faraz before he could ask.

"I was going to ask if you wanted a Twix," he said.

I grinned. He handed me the bar he'd been hiding in his pocket.

"I hear the community is still active," Faraz said. "Waiting for your father, or for someone to take his place."

Faraz seemed about to say something more but stopped. I felt suddenly irritated. Mishail always said that you had to verify three things before having any interest in a man. He had to be at least two years older, attractive, and of the right horoscope. Everything else could be negotiated. But Mishail's accounting missed some pretty important qualities. For example, being able to have a conversation with a girl like a normal human. Not being in jail, headed for jail, or thinking about making life choices that would lead to jail, like talking about my father's "community" of rebels.

"Your voice," Faraz said. "You have your father's voice."

I frowned.

"I don't mean that you sound like a man. Just that you both speak the same way."

"And how's that?"

"As if you're commanding an army," Faraz said.

I looked away, landing on the various SAT and TOEFL

books scattered everywhere. The school world of boys was actually pretty similar to ours. By law, the boys' school had to be at least five kilometers from ours to prevent the ever-troublesome potential indecency. But boys had to study the same things, take the same tests, and try for the same scholarships.

"My father says I must go abroad to study," Faraz said. "What about you? What are your scores?"

I did a double take. I wasn't used to such direct questions. Girls were more subtle. None of them would admit that they studied at all or that they were trying for universities that might not accept them. At most, they might ask if a test had gone well, and even if you'd aced it, you had to say you did just okay or the others would think you were being proud, which was worse than being stupid.

"If people knew you were trying for something, they might try for it, too, or cast an evil eye," Aisha always said. She wrote *Bismillah-ur-Rahman-ur-Rahim* at the top of all her tests to ward off bad luck.

I said, "I haven't got the scores back yet. But I don't want to leave the country."

"Why not?" Faraz asked. "Many universities offer scholarships, and with your brains, you'd easily get one."

It was none of his business. So easy for men to just set out on their adventures, leave everyone else behind. Even if I could leave, even if every cell in my body ached for scholarships that I wouldn't get, what was I supposed to do, abandon Mishail and my mother? Give up on my father?

I said the words I'd heard my father say a hundred times: "Better a prisoner in your own house than a guest in someone else's."

Faraz's face cleared, as if he'd just received some great revelation in my answer. The doorbell rang, and he went to answer it. I tiptoed to the closed door where my mother was talking to Hossein and his wife.

From beyond the thick wooden doors came a high-pitched noise that nearly made my heart stop. My mother was crying as if her heart had just been broken, a terrible, gut-wrenching sound.

I should have stayed to learn more, but I couldn't bear to hear it for another second. I backed away from the door and returned to the sofa in a daze. I'd been sitting there a few minutes when Faraz returned and said, "Looks like they're done."

Sure enough, the great wooden doors were open, and the three adults were coming out. I was glad my mother was wearing her veil, covering even her eyes. I didn't want to see the answers I knew I'd see, and I certainly didn't want Faraz to see her like that. Not that he would say anything, but still.

"So you managed to find us!" Hossein said, looking as if he'd been through a sleepless night. "Good girl, good girl. You take care of your mother now, you hear me?"

I nodded, irritated that he thought I wasn't already doing that.

"And you're studying hard? Your mother says you're going to study accounting, help her out with the catering business."

"Law," I said through my teeth. My mother's disapproval seeped through the veil.

"Same thing, of course," Hossein said obliviously. "Law and business, all about numbers. Sorting out inheritance, that sort of thing. Quick, what's three hundred and ninety-five times three?"

"One thousand, one hundred and eighty-five."

Hossein made a sound of amazed appreciation and asked a few more questions. "Any time you want a job here, it's yours," he said, laughing. "You can be my accountant, or maybe tutor this boy of mine in exchange for some"—he coughed discreetly as he whispered the word *driving* so only I would hear—"lessons."

Faraz blushed, and I gave Hossein a grudging smile.

"But no, that would be holding you back. You'll go far, no question about it. I think you're even sharper than your father was!"

Hossein must have realized from my expression that he'd said something wrong, because his voice fell to a mumble, and he showed us out. I walked briskly home alongside my mother. I wanted to ask, *What's going on? What were you guys talking about?* But we'd stopped talking to each other long ago about anything except the basic necessities of life.

I hate you, I'd said.

Grow up. Stop sulking as if I'm the reason he's gone, and stop acting like a baby. I can't take care of both of us right now.

Fine. I don't need you anyway.

My heart burned and pulsed, a sun bereft of its planets.

5

HIJRA

Faraz was right. The tension couldn't last, and never did. But in Saudi Arabia, change always came with the sudden violence of a sandstorm, so that when it was over, you couldn't even remember what used to be, and you certainly had no time to grieve.

One day I woke up panting from a nightmare in which I'd overslept and missed a test. I had overslept, but there was no missed test. The news reporter, with her plastic face that shone out from the *hijab*, insisted that everything was fine, that the National Guard was out in full force, ensuring the safety of all citizens.

"You have to learn how to read her face, not just listen to her words," my mother said, squeezing my shoulders in uncharacteristic affection. "She's terrified."

So the latest in the line of cave-dwelling fanatics had declared that the reopening of KAUST under the protection of the American military was a sign of the final decline and humiliation of the Muslim world and had to be avenged at any cost.

"We just can't win," Fatima Aunty said, rocking back and forth. "Women aren't allowed to work alongside men because they wouldn't be safe from harassment. So we open a coed university to train people and that gets closed because of terrorist threats. We reopen it, and now *all* girls' schools are under threat. What do they want us to do, crawl under a rock and wait to die?"

"Yes," my mother said, her chuckle so bitter it made me shudder. "Or move to Hofuf and eat cockroaches."

It was her long-running joke when she was frustrated that we'd move to Hofuf, where the late King Abdullah had set up a walled city for women alone. It was rumored that out there in the middle of nowhere, Palestinian refugees and Yemeni ex-prostitutes survived on rats and desert locusts.

For the rest of the day the news on Channel 1, the free public station Mishail affectionately called "Butt-Kiss TV," showed nonstop footage of royalty and government ministers, including Mishail's father, walking to and from the *Majlis Al-Shura* with smiling faces.

Everything's fine, see?

But on Al Jazeera, which we got because of our neighbor's illegal but hidden satellite dish, young boys chased after school buses with darkened windows in the Rowdah district, throwing rocks at the panes. "Stop stealing our jobs, ugly bitches!" one of them shouted at the camera in English. I flinched, not used to hearing curses flung so casually. Another young man came up to the first and threw an arm around him.

The reporter asked him in English, "Are you also concerned about the high unemployment rate among Saudi youth?"

The second man blinked in confusion. He said, "If they get jobs, they don't want to marry. They want too much *mahr*. Blackmail is un-Islamic!"

The two young men chanted that last in unison.

"She shouldn't be watching this," Fatima Aunty said to my mother.

"It's okay," I said. "I'm leaving."

When my mind refused to quiet, I phoned Mishail. Naturally, we couldn't talk about what was actually happening, but I just needed to hear her voice.

"What are you up to?" I asked. "Just talk, okay?"

"You know my window, the one in my room?" Mishail said.

"Yes?"

"I found out recently that the style of it is called a *harem* window," Mishail said, laughing. "It's the old Hejazi style, for, uh, those kinds of women to see out into the street and call over men they liked."

"Because you can see out, but you can't see in," I said,

remembering the decorative wooden shutters and the broad sill that allowed someone to sit and look down into the street without being seen.

"Exactly. So I've been sitting naked at my window for the last two hours. I can feel the breeze against my skin, but no one can see me. Ha!"

I laughed so hard tears came to my eyes. No matter how bad a situation got, you could always trust Mishail to find a way to laugh, to make a joke about it, to rebel quietly against fathers and *muttaween* and teachers and anyone else who got in her way.

I held the phone tightly, glad Mishail wasn't expecting me to speak.

Things seemed to settle in the way they always did. The government made a concession to the religious authorities that would reassure them . . . until the next scandal. When they announced that KASP scholarships would no longer be available to women except when no acceptable male candidate could be found, I started laughing. I felt I'd expected it, that it was what had choked me up on the phone with Mishail. Not what had already happened, but what I knew would have to happen next to restore peace.

Schools—most of them—reopened on Saturday, after being closed for a week. Armed guards were stationed outside the gates, which meant no more sneaking out to get ice cream. The second floor had broken windows, the ones high enough for rocks thrown over the brick walls to reach a target. The name of the school, Nizamiyyah Secondary, once so prominent that it was visible three blocks down, had been painted over completely.

Most disturbing of all, new girls at the school had green uniforms instead of blue, and stared at us warily like hunted animals. Speakers had been installed in the hallways, and Maryam Madam's voice rang out over them as she called a special assembly.

We snapped out of our chairs, years of practice helping us to don our *abayas* and veils and form the requisite line in a matter of seconds. Aisha was the shortest, at the front of the line, her eyes wide with worry. Behind her stood Mishail, with her arms on Aisha's shoulders, elbows bent like a compressed spring. Once we were in the hallway, the spring lengthened as the girls took the required one-arm distance from one another. Similar lines emerged from other doors, and the girls in the classroom closest to the fire escape were already on their way down the stairs. In single file, we marched, shoving one another gently. People kept whispering, "What do you think this is about?" and "Leena, you must know. You always know everything."

I didn't know, and the uncertainty was driving me insane.

In the auditorium, Maryam Madam coughed into the microphone. With a great thundering, an auditorium full of girls clicked their black buckled heels together and stood up straight and silent.

"My dear girls, I want to start by saying how glad I am that you are here with us today. Our numbers have shrunk in the last few days, for reasons you know well. Your teachers and I would like nothing better than to shield you from the things that happen outside these walls, things that should not be your concern. The last few days have been trying for all of us, but probably most for the students and staff of Najd National School. They could not return to their own campus, and so we welcome them to join us and share what we have."

Thunderous applause broke out in the auditorium, along with cheers and completely inappropriate whistles. Mishail turned around from the front of the line and caught my gaze. My chest seized up with nearly unbearable happiness. *This*. This was why I wouldn't want to leave, even if it were possible. Where else would you find a community that would bear you up in disaster without question or hesitation, asking nothing in return?

"At this time," Maryam Madam said, "let me remind you of the prophet's own journey, the one that began our history and is at the heart of our values as a community, as a people. Life in Mecca had become unendurable for Muhammad (peace be upon him). His own family and friends threatened to kill him. After days in the hot desert, he landed in Medina and was given shelter. The people of Medina welcomed him into their hearts, trusted him so much that they asked him to be their adjudicator when the tribes began quarreling. In his name, I ask you to take our newest guests into your hearts, to trust your sisters in these troubled times."

Sofia whispered in my ear, "Why would we not trust them?"

I shrugged and strained to see the headmistress's face. She seemed anxious. I noticed something I should've seen before. Next to her stood a woman clad head to toe in a gray *jellaba*. It had no embroidery of any kind. Her face had neither crow's-feet nor wrinkles, and her mouth, completely without even the slightest gloss, was the same lifeless color as her skin. Her eyes, the only signs of life, were two black marbles that darted around the auditorium restlessly.

Maryam Madam said, "And with that, I invite the headmistress of Najd National to say a few words."

She stepped back from the microphone. The woman in the gray *jellaba* took a step forward and grabbed it.

If I hadn't been watching Maryam Madam so carefully, I would have missed the cloud of worry that passed over her face. It was gone almost immediately.

"Hello, girls," said the woman. Her voice quavered, with nervousness or emotion I couldn't tell. "You can call me Naseema Madam. I was the headmistress of Najd National until recently. I want to thank you all, particularly Maryam here, for the warm welcome."

Maryam Madam's shoulders relaxed slightly.

"I wanted to take a moment to address my girls, to comfort them in this difficult time, but to be honest, I wasn't sure what to say. I'm not as great a speaker as Maryam, whose words flow faster than the rivers of Jordan."

There was nervous laughter. I wondered whether Naseema Madam was just a bad speaker or if she had meant to insult Maryam Madam in some way.

"Maryam's discussion of the *hijra* helped me find some words. I want to tell my girls that the way forward is not by complaining about the unfairness of what has happened to us. To complain is to question the will of God. In times like this, our faith becomes more important than ever. Back at Najd National, we held ourselves to high standards in all respects. Some of our teachers were men, so we showed discipline in our dress, in our daily prayers, and in our studies. We showed modesty in our attire and in our accomplishments. We will continue to do this here and earn the respect of our hosts. Do I make myself clear?"

There was silence in the hall. We at Nizamiyyah had never been spoken to like this, as if we were six-year-olds. And one of the rare pleasures of an all-girls school was that we didn't have to wear our *abaya* and *hijab* indoors, when we were among only other women. Did she really expect her girls to stay veiled even inside?

"What a *garawiyya!*" Sofia said. The word meant a woman who was backward, who had arrived straight from the village.

I chuckled. To my surprise, Maryam Madam heard us. Her eyes sparked with a fury I had never seen, and certainly never seen directed at *me*.

She took the microphone back from Naseema Madam.

"We have much to learn from our new friends," she said, and her eyes were still fixed on me. "Although some of you are newer than others, I want you to know that you will be treated fairly and equally at this school. Naseema here is not my *guest*, she is a headmistress of this school as much as I am. An insult to her is an insult to me."

I shifted on my feet guiltily. Maryam Madam must have seen it, because she relaxed, and her voice became softer.

She said, "When Muhammad heard the call of the angel Jibrail on Mount Hira, he was not a young man. He didn't want his life to change. He had wealth, fame, a wife . . . all of which had been difficult to acquire because he was an orphan. He'd built himself up out of nothing. And yet, at the age of *fifty-two*, he started over. Not many people could survive something like that. None of you children can understand what it means to survive something like that. But life in Mecca had become impossible. It's true that he escaped persecution and found hospitality in Medina. It's true that all *hijra* means these days is safety from physical danger. But Muhammad brought something more to that first *hijra*. Starting over takes courage, a special kind of courage that people lose as they get older, or when they have more to lose than to gain by giving up their old ways. Naseema and her girls have shown great courage in coming to us. So I'd like my girls to honor it by opening your hearts to these women who are strong but not hard, who are able to adapt without losing their religion, and who are willing to move forward without growing bitter. Can you girls do that for me?"

There was silence. Most of the girls in the auditorium were either crying, nodding, or both. I was digging my nails into my palms and clenching my teeth, unable to cope with the shame that threatened to drag me out to sea.

6

FAISALIYAH

Two days later, I realized that Mishail had gone completely mad. To be fair, Mishail had always been a little mad. But this special blend of constantly trembling lips and utterly insane plans was brand new and had everything to do with the new girl in our class, Daria Abulkhair.

"Let's be extra nice to her," I'd said the day of the assembly, inspired by Maryam Madam's speech and seeing Daria's solitary green uniform in our sea of blue. "Joining a new school in senior year? I wouldn't wish that on anyone."

It turned out (naturally) Mishail had already adopted the new girl. Daria was half American and top of her class, and she had just been selected to emcee a weekend TV show for kids.

"Stuffed-puppet show or funny-voices show?" I asked.

Mishail shoved me in the ribs. "You said be nice!"

Law class began. Batool Madam pointed Daria to a seat in the front row.

"I don't know what you've been told about our school," Batool Madam said. "But I don't like style without substance. You have to really know your material. And I don't tolerate any smart talk, you hear me? I'm keeping an eye on you."

Daria raised a hand. "Are we allowed to ask questions?"

"Of course," Batool Madam said, but then added, "But not so many that you're distracting the other girls. This is not your time to catch up. If you're falling behind, just read the textbook quietly and get help from the others later. Now, all of you, turn to the chapter on marriage. *And no laughing!* This is a serious, important subject. What are you going to use for the rest of your life, this or your silly variables x and y?"

Nervous giggles broke out. Mishail and I glanced at each other, unable to contain our excitement. *Finally!* It was only in senior year that we were allowed to learn about marriage, and we'd already read the entire chapter as soon as the textbooks arrived.

"Read quietly until page one fifty, and then I'll ask questions."

"It's a shame the textbook doesn't say anything useful about *getting* a husband," Mishail whispered. "It's just obey this, inherit that."

Sofia turned slightly in her seat so she could talk to us. "I bet the new girl knows a thing or two about boys. We should ask her if she's met any. In American schools, girls and boys study together."

"How does anyone get any studying done?" Mishail asked. "I'm serious!"

"What's your sun sign, Mishail?" Sofia asked.

"Leo," Mishail and I said together.

"And Leena's a Scorpio, no wonder you guys mix so well. Fire and water. I only asked because my sister-in-law is Egyptian. She says there's a way older than sun signs that works better for girls, to take your name and your mother's name and use that to find your true soul mate."

"Will you guys SHUT UP?" Bilquis hissed, covering her ears. "It's bad enough that you're into all the *haraam* things, do you have to corrupt everyone else as well with your stupid stuperstitions?"

Mishail and I burst into quiet laughter. "Stuperstitions!" we whispered together.

"What's going on there?" Batool Madam asked. "Mishail! Done reading? Please list the requirements for a valid marriage."

"Consent of the bride and her guardian," Mishail said, blushing furiously. "The contract with the *mahr* to be paid to the woman, agreed to by both parties. Two witnesses."

"And?"

Mishail swallowed but said nothing. I kept my gaze in front of me but started writing on my desk. *CHASTITY*.

"Eyes up here, don't look at your book!" Batool Madam said. "No?"

This was usually when she asked, *Anyone else?* I raised one hand and drummed my fingertips on the table to draw the teacher's attention. Once I gave the answer, Mishail would be off the hook.

"How about you, new girl? Think you know the answer?"

I gasped softly. It wasn't fair to do this to anyone on her first day. I raised my hand even higher.

"No, I want Miss Abulkhair to show us what she knows."

Daria stood up and said in a voice that was completely calm and confident, "In addition to the consent of the woman, preventing a forced marriage, sufficient *mahr* for her to independently survive a husband's death or divorce, and a contract witnessed by at least two Muslims, both parties must be chaste."

It was so silent in the classroom I thought I could hear Batool Madam's blood draining from her pale face. True, Daria's Arabic was a little artificial, but her answer was perfect. I felt a wave of triumph pulsing through my fingers and toes. The thought *Finally!* occurred to me, as if I'd been in some tough battle and someone had come to help me at long last.

"Not bad," Batool Madam said. "Did you have a good law teacher in your other school?"

"We had a *halaqa* system," Daria said. She hesitated, as if about to explain but not until she was asked.

"I've heard of that. It's the one where you sit in a circle or something, yes?"

"Yes," Daria said. "It's the same system that they used in Qaraouine. We sat in a circle around our teacher and had a debate, for instance, about whether the silence of a woman counts as consent. Al-Bukhari says it does, but Binti Khudam had her marriage annulled by the prophet because she'd been too shy to refuse."

There it was again, the absolute silence.

"Peace be upon him," Daria added hastily, and I grinned. I was really going to like this girl, who knew of Qaraouine, the first university in the world, the one built by a woman but now closed to them, this girl who could manage Batool the Fool as well as I could.

"I see," Batool Madam said coldly. She scanned Daria from head to toe and said, "Next question. Let's see. You, in the third row. What are the rules of *khula*? Mishail, you can sit down now."

I breathed a sigh of relief. The storm had passed. When Batool Madam was in retreat and licking her wounds, she picked on the girls whose names she didn't know, the ones who scared easily. I pointed at the word *chastity* written on my desk, and Mishail began scratching it out as a girl in the third row stammered the rules by which a woman could petition for a divorce as long as she approached the court with an appropriate male relative.

Once Batool Madam left the classroom, we gathered around Daria. We usually had five minutes of peace between classes while teachers switched rooms. It was a simple system; the girls of a class had usually been together since they'd started school at the age of three and had to take all the same subjects. The routine for seniors was intense, with two classes before the *zuhr* prayer, followed by lunch and three more subjects, taking us almost all the way to the sunset *maghreb*. Only then did the buses and drivers take us home.

Despite gathering around Daria with intense curiosity, nobody seemed to know what questions to ask the new girl. Mishail spoke first, with a flawlessly casual flick of her headscarf. "What you did today was really cool."

"It's nothing," Daria said, grinning mischievously. "I didn't know how far to push her, you know? She was so funny, pretending she knew what a *halaqa* system was, as if sitting around a fire singing songs is the same thing as having a debate."

I laughed and said, "The easiest way past her is with some piece of information she doesn't know. It's like cheese to a rat."

"I'll keep that in mind for next time," Daria said. "I have all sorts of juicy tidbits about *zawaj al-misyar*."

I frowned. Decent girls didn't talk about concubine marriages. Someone behind me drew in a sharp breath.

"Traveler's marriage? Sometimes known as temporary marriage?" Daria asked. "Oh, it's too funny. It's a way for single women to find a convenient guardian, or to, you know, *do things*, without waiting. Understand?"

Mishail laughed, but I only smiled uncomfortably.

"There's even a website, where all these Saudi women try to find good men from Yemen or Oman to have a *misyar* marriage with so they can live in peace, maybe have a little fun."

"That's disgusting," Bilquis said. "Saudi women would never do such shameful things. You're lying."

I blinked, unable to decide how I felt. My stomach agreed with Bilquis, which was disgusting in and of itself. My head agreed with Daria. If all you had to do to live in peace was sign a piece of paper, it was a tempting idea.

"I think it's perfectly reasonable that given a terrible situation, people will do whatever they need to do to survive," Mishail said, making peace again. "Isn't that what you always say, Leena? Water will find a way."

I exhaled slowly, glaring at Mishail in warning. The phrase was "A river carves its own route," said by Abdullah Al-Hamid, the famous freedom fighter. But it wasn't safe to talk about him here, in front of Bilquis.

"You would say that," Bilquis said. "Neither of you are

exactly role models for good character, are you? Like father, like daughter."

"What's that supposed to mean?" I said.

"Teacher's coming!" Aisha called, and we flew back to our seats.

As the chemistry teacher walked in, Sofia passed Mishail a note. Mishail opened it and placed it in the middle so I could see.

If you guys want to bring the Almighty Bilquis down from her righteous cloud, I'd be happy to help. :-)—D.

"You're right," Mishail said, folding the paper up neatly and stuffing it in her bra. "I like her."

AT THE TIME, I had fought the strange curdling in my belly as paranoia.

Now, banging my head against the coffee table at home, I wondered how Mishail could have turned into a crazy person in less than forty-eight hours. I closed my eyes, holding the phone to my ear as Mishail went on to podcast an episode of Daria's biography.

Daria lives in one of those American ARAMCO campuses where they have a swimming pool and no Al-Hai'a.

Daria learned to drive in New York. She once drove the wrong way down a one-way street and had to reverse while a bus came at her!

Daria's father is out on business trips all the time, so she has her own personal driver from Pakistan!

Daria, Daria, Daria!

And then the call to end them all. Mishail's voice sounded choked up, and at first, my pulse raced, thinking something had happened, maybe the minister had finally gone too far, but no.

"Daria has kissed a boy before," Mishail said, sounding as if she might cry for jealousy. "*French*-kissed. With tongue."

"Mishy, someone might be listening to this phone call."

"Are *you* listening to *me*? She has *experience*. And it wasn't on one of her American vacations, either. It was here. She says the easiest way to meet boys is in Faisaliyah. It's complicated, but we can do it. We have to."

"Do you have any idea how insane you sound?" I whispered. "This isn't like wearing red on Valentine's Day or listening to music at school. You're talking expelled, head-shaved-by-police, go-to-*jail* dangerous. We can't talk about this on the phone. Think about what your father would say if he heard you."

"You're right," Mishail said, and sniffled. "I hate my life. I hate everything. We're not even really living, are we? What's the point of it all? We should just—"

"Okay, stop that," I said hastily, knowing how this particular thread of conversation ended. Stupid *Hunger Games* books, which gave Mishail the idea of collective suicide as a form of protest.

"Leena, I think my father wants to marry me off at the end of this year," Mishail said, crying. "He won't tell me anything about it, but I hear him with his friends, and my name comes up. Why else would my name come up? He's going to sell me for my *mahr*, I know it. And then we'll never see each other again. If that happens, I'll—"

"No, you won't," I said. The important thing was never to let Mishail finish any of her sentences. It was like using tissues to direct the course of spilled water, building dams as Mishail's emotions explored all possible outlets. "No matter what happens, I won't leave you. You hear me?"

"I just have this feeling," Mishail said, hiccuping now, "that this is the end, you know? Our last year together. You're going to go to university, and I'm going to end up married to some old buffoon with bad teeth who smells like garlic and stale musk."

I bit the inside of my cheek to keep from laughing. But it was no use.

"You're laughing, aren't you? You are!"

"It won't happen, Mishy. You know as well as I do that if you say no, you can't be married off against your will. It's against the law. Just keep saying no, and we'll be fine. I'm not going anywhere, and neither are you."

"So you'll come with us?"

"With who? Where?"

"Faisaliyah!" Mishail said, her voice rising to a whine. "If I can find someone reasonably good before my father settles things, I'll feel better. I don't want to feel like I have no options."

"Mishy, men aren't teddy bears," I said, pinching my temples. *When you depend on them, they get arrested or leave.* "Besides, I have to study."

"I thought you said you weren't going to foreign schools."

"I'm not."

"Then why do you care? Eighty percent is good enough to get into Princess Nora. You only need the really high scores to go abroad. This is my *life*, Leena!"

"Okay, okay," I said, knowing I had to go if only to get Mishail out of inevitable trouble. "I'll come."

THE TRIP TO Faisaliyah was an unmitigated disaster.

Even ordinarily, I hated malls. They were an overstimulating mashup of Swatch, Swarovski, and Starbucks, to the point where even the chlorinated and multicolored water of the marble fountains sounded like the clink of coins. And Faisaliyah—with its air conditioners growling at full blast, the red-carpet treatment women got as they entered, valets opening doors, and chauffeurs sitting in the distance hoping for a glimpse of a high-heeled ankle underneath the train of black silk—just wasn't my idea of fun. Other girls loved malls, lived for the day they could enter Il Terrazzo, the mixed-gender restaurant at the top of the tower, on the arm of a husband. They practiced their walk at home so they could be seen at the mall, carrying large designer handbags over their black *abayas* to tease the exiled men, and then demonstrating their style to the women inside.

I didn't know what I'd expected, but Daria acting as tour guide to the mall Mishail and I had grown up in was not it. And worse was the way Mishail acted around her, as if Daria might know a little bit about boys, but she, Mishail, had all the ancient wisdom of Arab womanhood behind her proclamations of who was "dressed deadly" and who was "just dead." As if it were a great bedouin secret that nail polish kept stocking tears from running. As if using lemon and glycerin to bleach your skin into fairness were something women of the desert had done for millennia, rather than a stupid fashion trend that came about from watching smuggled American movies with white women in them.

There was no way for all three of us to walk in a row, so Mishail had her arm linked through Daria's "to make her feel welcome," leaving me trailing them like a sulky child.

Upon Daria's insistence, we bought small, perfumed calling cards and sat down at the Starbucks to fill them out.

"Just a name and a phone number or e-mail address. It doesn't have to be your real name if you're only looking for fun, and even for serious men, they'll understand if you explain when you're ready that you didn't give your real name."

I got up to go to the bathroom, mostly to buy some

time and avoid explaining that I wasn't really interested in hunting for boys. Even if I did find a guy I liked, what would be the point? Sooner or later he'd find out about my unfortunate situation and nothing would come of it except humiliation and heartbreak. This whole idea reeked of the kind of danger I had no use for. This wasn't like climbing onto the roof of the portable cabin at school to see over the ten-foot wall that held us in. At worst, you'd fall and break a bone or two. This kind of adventure could leave you shattered, like the beggar women in the slums of Naseem who trembled and muttered to themselves because their husbands had abandoned them.

When I returned, Mishail said, "Hey, Leena, do you know Bilquis's phone number?"

"Yeah, why?"

"Daria had a really great idea for how to teach her a lesson."

"Mishy," I said, but I knew how this would go. Mishail pouted. I wrote the number on one of the cards. I saw Mishail and Daria exchange glances. "What are you going to do?"

"Nothing," Mishail said.

"Don't worry," Daria said, entering the number into her phone. "I'm going to become Bilquis's new best friend."

I scowled. I turned to Mishail, expecting to see an explanation or the same suspicion there. What I saw instead unnerved me. Mishail was gazing at Daria with open adoration, as if Daria had constructed all the colored fountains and marble cathedrals of Faisaliyah herself, just to make Mishail smile.

On the way out of the mall, as we headed toward the parking garage where the driver was waiting, Daria said, "Wait a sec."

We had caught the attention of four young boys who were smoking by a pillar, boys who were clearly waiting to catch a glimpse of any women who might be at the mall. Daria looked left and right, as if she were crossing the street, and then whipped off her headscarf, letting her waist-length hair down for a second. She bundled it back up quickly, jabbed in a pen to hold the knot together, and retied her headscarf, never once looking at the boys, who watched her in silent awe.

We continued to the car. Since I was a step behind Daria and Mishail, I saw that each of them casually let slip a calling card that fluttered to the ground. The two of them never looked back, but I did, and I saw the boys run over to the space the girls had vacated, wrestling one another for the cards as if they were gold coins dropped by queens.

7

WASTA

On the eighth of October, Mishail and I were sitting on the ledge outside the second-floor bathroom window, the hiding spot we'd discovered the year before when I finally grew tall enough to climb to it and help Mishail up. The ledge overlooked the brick wall, which was nearly a foot thick. The broken glass that covered it sparkled innocently in the sunshine, as if it weren't the reason our school was still standing after the riots when so many others were not.

Mishail blew out a stream of soap bubbles. I aimed the pellet gun and shot them down in quick succession.

The pellets were foam darts the size of a pencil eraser, and a bag of a thousand usually got us through an hour, or a single class. The darts landed in the empty lot on the other side of the school wall, far from the road or prying religious eyes.

"You can't keep claiming you aren't upset," Mishail said. "Your aim is always better when you're angry."

I said nothing. I could still hear the echoes of Daria's shriek of joy when she was named one of the two members on the debate team who would compete for the *Majlis* internship. Mishail had squeezed my hand when her name was announced as the second candidate.

"I didn't have anything to do with the choice," she said now. "I know it should be you there, not me. Don't you think everyone knows that?"

I couldn't speak. If I tried, I knew I'd start crying. I looked at the bubble blower expectantly. Mishail sighed into the lens, and a large, watery bubble came out of the other side. I narrowed my eyes and shot it.

"It's not fair," I said finally. "She's half American. She can go anywhere anytime."

"It's not that simple. Her mother's American, not her father, so she's as stuck as we are. They're not that rich. Besides, you're not actually angry *she* was chosen."

Even I had to admit that Daria would be great at the debate. And what kind of friend would I be if I wasn't happy that Mishail was getting the opportunity of a lifetime?

"At least Bilquis got put in her place," Mishail said.

Despite my disappointment, I grinned. Daria was

72

smooth, that was for sure. She had spent a week worshipping at the altar of Bilquis, sitting beside her, phoning her every evening, putting on a campaign that would have melted the desert rocks, never mind Bilquis's stony heart. Then Daria's candidacy for the debate was announced, and she was the unchallenged queen of Nizamiyyah. Younger girls turned their heads to look at her in awe, older girls with envy, and today at lunch Bilquis walked up to take her rightful place beside Daria and Mishail in front of everyone.

She never made it. The whispers and pointed fingers and laughter stopped her dead in her tracks. I had been watching by Mishail's side, and Mishail showed me her cell phone, hidden in sandwich paper. Bilquis's deepest, darkest secrets were all online for anyone in Daria's now expansive social network to see.

Bilquis had shit her pants in the first grade, too shy to ask the male teacher for permission to go to the bathroom.

Bilquis's mother was terrified that she might be seen by non-*mahram* men, so she carried around some breast milk in a vial, presumably to force it down the throat of any male who caught her unawares, making them *rada*, or permitted to her.

Bilquis had spent the rest of lunch crying and was now wearing her *niqab* in the classroom to cover her tearstained face.

I kicked out from the ledge, dissatisfied and confused.

If I were a truly good person, I'd be happy for Daria and Mishail. If I were a truly evil person, I'd have taken more pleasure in Bilquis's getting what she deserved.

The bell rang. We left our equipment on the ledge for next time. I helped Mishail through the window, laughing at the romantic picture we made when Mishail landed in my arms.

"You're so strong," Mishail said in a fake voice, her arms going around my neck. "My hero."

"That's me, fighting off the evil soap bubbles of Riyadh, keeping us from getting sticky."

"There you are. If you two are done fooling around, Leena, I need to see you in my office. *Now.*"

I let Mishail down and wiped my hands guiltily as I followed the headmistress. Maryam Madam was upset about something. And she clearly had been for a while, because as soon as we got into the office and closed the door, the headmistress went straight into Phase Three, as if expecting me to catch up.

"I'm not even surprised anymore when this stuff happens, just disappointed," the headmistress said, pacing the small space so fast she made me dizzy. "I spent all this time trying to understand the loopholes of the system. To even apply for that internship, you'd need your father's permission. So I wrote to him, and I wrote to the authorities. I called in favors. I did all but use the Sudairi card, because you never know what could happen when you blast that bomb."

I blinked, trying to keep up. I had heard the rumor that Maryam Madam was one of the Sudairi women, almost as powerful as the Sudairi men. Sure, the *Economist* and the *New York Times* had written articles glorifying the Sudairi Seven, the full-blooded brothers of the royal line who acted as a single political bloc, using their influence, or *wasta*, to shape the country and leave it to their blood-sons. The articles never spoke of the women, not even of Hassa Al-Sudairi, the most powerful queen in our country's history, the one whom the country's founder was so obsessed with he married her *twice*.

"Finally, *finally*, I got a court order that says in matters of education, until your father is out of prison, my guardian can function as yours, so all I needed to do was get my eleven-year-old to sign a blank sheet of paper—he likes signing things, it makes him feel important—and then I only found out today that since our schools were merged, Naseema and I could submit only one team to this debate."

I didn't know what to say. I was torn between being touched at the headmistress's thoughtfulness and outraged at the thought that my educational future was in the hands of an eleven-year-old boy I'd never met. I fought off the bitter laughter that was now second nature every time I discovered exactly how badly my country was broken.

The headmistress's gaze grew softer, more calculating.

"I know, I know," she said. "I know this is disappointing, but I want you to trust me. If our team wins, the minister will gladly give Mishail's share to the school. All the parents of Daria's classmates who stopped sending their daughters to school might realize there's hope if Daria wins. I have to admit it was a brilliant idea from Naseema, balancing the half American with the minister's daughter, so nobody can attack Daria's character!"

I swallowed hard to hide my sense of betrayal. All this time, I had thought that Maryam Madam had somehow been outwitted by the crow from Najd National, who had wanted to put her girl first. But no, Maryam Madam had agreed to choose Daria over me. Why did I have to make all the sacrifices?

"Tell you what, Leena. I won't stop trying to help you, because I know you'll hold on. These other girls? They haven't a lick of street sense. They may be smart, but they aren't *clever*, and every one of them fancies themselves the next Manal Al-Sharif."

I squirmed. *Of course* every girl wanted to be Manal, that queen of the rebellion who had become so famous during the Arab Spring for inciting women to break the law and drive. Like her, every girl wanted to drive around Riyadh with lipstick and sunglasses, making snarky comments to their best friend in the passenger seat who was filming a video that would spread around the world and set fire to a revolution.

"You and I know better, don't we?" the headmistress said, placing a hand on my cheek.

I closed my eyes and leaned into the touch.

"Yes," I said. My voice was hoarse, as if I'd been the one ranting this whole time. I said the words the headmistress had once used to get through to me, let them soothe the deep hurt that had been gnawing at me all day.

"Anger puts you in jail; patience lets you prevail."

8

SHOUFA

*I*n the middle of home economics class, I saw Daria pass Mishail a note. Mishail's eyes widened upon reading it, and she started turning pages in the novel hidden inside her textbook.

I struggled with myself, torn between wanting to know what the two of them were up to and not wanting to seem pathetic by asking. Mishail patted my arm urgently and handed over the book she was reading.

The book was *Love, Lies, and Leila Baxter,* in which two unbelievably stupid girls, Leila and Mabel, somehow got into college even though they barely got Bs in school and cried a lot over boys who were even stupider than they were. I skimmed the book, trying to understand why

Mishail had passed it to me. Mishail passed me Daria's note, which just said *120*. So I skipped to that page, where Leila met a guy named Mike, who she kept saying was thrilling even though he'd done nothing thrilling beyond wear a black motorcycle jacket. But on the right page, Leila went back to his dorm room with him and lost her virginity.

My eyes flew wide open, and I nearly dropped the book. My shock was mirrored in Mishail's eyes. We had never read a book with s-e-x in it before. The censors meticulously screened every book, CD, and DVD, erasing all bad words, kisses, and nudity. Even the biology textbooks were covered in black censorship ink, never mind novels and magazines.

Mishail jerked her head, and I read on. In the next chapter, Leila decided she was too young to be tied down, so she dumped Mike and moved on to someone else who was even more thrilling.

I felt a headache coming on. At the end of the class, when the teacher left the room, Daria turned to face us.

"Well?" she asked.

"You're right," Mishail said. "I can't believe it."

"Right about what?" I asked.

Daria said nothing, just raised her eyebrows at Mishail.

"She's not going to tell on us," Mishail said. "She's not like that."

"What can't you believe?" I asked Mishail.

"The love scenes, of course!" Mishail said, louder than she'd intended, because she immediately clapped a hand over her mouth.

Too late. We had an audience, and Zainab and Iman, two girls who sat within earshot, turned around to listen.

"I wish we could go somewhere private," Daria said with a sigh, but she didn't seem to mean it, because she explained to the eavesdroppers, "We're just discussing a book."

Mishail asked in a low voice, "Do girls in America really do it before they're married? With multiple people?"

Zainab and Iman gasped in unison.

"*Wah*, you girls are so sheltered and innocent!" Daria said, shaking her head. "In America, people do it all the time in college. Many of them even start in high school. And everybody drinks. It's totally normal. It's their body, so it's their choice."

She spoke with all the authority of having lived in New York and gone to an American school before her family moved here. I felt a flush of shame and wondered whether Daria had intended to make us feel small.

"Normal?" Mishail cried. "But how do their parents allow it?"

"Leave their parents, how do *they* think that's okay, to even *think* such dirty things!" Iman said.

I said nothing because I only vaguely knew about sex. The book was full of "hard muscles" and "fierce kisses," but it gave no practical information about exactly what happened between a man and a woman.

"Oh my God," Daria said, her strange accent drawing out the words, as if she had to speak slowly to make us village idiots understand. "Anyway, now you know what really happens out there. *Of course* people have sex before marriage. Not just in America; here, too."

There was a loud hiss, and Iman covered her ears.

Daria shook her head and said, "Whatever. Even if you wait, chances are your husband won't. You have to learn all the tricks, otherwise you'll be a stereotypical Saudi wife, lying there like a dead fish."

"Daria," asked little Zainab, "can I read the book next?"

Zainab's pale heart-shaped face was framed by the black *hijab* pulled tight around her head. Since we didn't have to wear a *hijab* inside the school, this was a sign of her religious piety, which made her request all the more weird. Why did a religious goody-goody want to read a book like that?

"I don't know," Daria said.

"It's okay," Zainab said, turning bright red. "It . . . it doesn't matter."

There was something about the way she said it that made Daria narrow her eyes.

"I'd be willing to make an exception, just this once. But only if there's a good reason."

"You can't tell anyone, but I'm engaged," Zainab said, not meeting anyone's eyes.

"Congrat—" Mishail began, but Zainab shook her head to keep her quiet.

"He comes from a very liberal family," Zainab continued. "When they came to see my parents for the *shoufa*, I was wearing my veil over my face. I was already so nervous that he would see my face and decide not to marry me, but then his parents said their son would not consent to the marriage unless he got to speak to the girl first, in private. My parents told me to wait in the study, and when he came in, he asked me to remove my veil."

"You didn't tell me that part!" Iman said. "Nobody can ask you to remove your veil. What kind of a Muslim is he?"

Zainab silenced her with a rather majestic wave of her hand. I marveled at it, as it approached Mishail's in dignity.

"I have nothing to hide from God or man," Zainab continued. "Besides, he said that a *shoufa* was supposed to be a *viewing* after all, and left it up to me. I removed my veil but left my hair covered. And, of course, we left the door open. He left after a few minutes, and later we learned that he consented to the marriage."

Zainab paused for a second and looked around as if to gauge the impression she was making. "He says that after the engagement, I should kiss him. When I told him I can't until we're married, he was really disappointed."

Still, I said nothing. While it was normal that girls who couldn't get into college would have to get married, Zainab was only fifteen. Was I next? God forbid.

"Who is he to demand something like that?" Iman asked. "He can't blackmail you!"

"He didn't! It's not like that. He's a really good man. He would never back out of the marriage or even say anything to me if I didn't. That's not the problem. I—I was wondering—"

"You want to kiss him, don't you?" Daria asked. Her tone was odd, almost jealous.

Zainab's silence confirmed this. Iman looked ready to cry.

"It's not dangerous, is it?" Zainab asked. "If it's just kissing? I don't know if it's wrong or not."

"I don't think it's wrong if you're engaged," Iman reassured her, rubbing circles on Zainab's back. Nobody else spoke. I wanted to say that even if it wasn't *wrong*, it was probably dangerous, because how would you be able to just stop at kissing? My mother had always said that boys were like cigarettes or drugs: once you got involved, you couldn't stop.

"It's not wrong," Daria declared, and Zainab sat up hopefully. "All right, you can have the book for now. But really, Zainab, you shouldn't be getting engaged so young. It's so backward."

Zainab flinched.

"I know you don't know any different," Daria said, "but girls should explore their options, not just be grateful that someone as old as their father is willing to marry them. You should have the self-respect to be willing to wait for true love." She rubbed Zainab's shoulder. "I'm sorry, I don't mean to hurt you, but—"

"Then why did you?" I snapped.

"Hey, I just tell it like it is. Tell the truth, do *you* really think it's right, Zainab's getting married at fifteen?"

I knew I was caught, but it made me only more furious. "If she were being forced into it, I'd help her get out of it. If she changed her mind later, I'd support a divorce. Her choices are her own."

I grabbed the book out of Zainab's hands.

"Even if you do go through with the marriage," I said to Zainab, shoving the book back at Daria, "you'll be happier if you're innocent. If you read this trash, you'll think you have to look like a supermodel and then give yourself up the first time the guy calls you *habibti*."

Those were my mother's words, not mine. Embarrassment made Zainab's face look like an overripe tomato. Seeing it, I felt a flush of irritation. Daria dangled the book over Zainab's still-outstretched hand.

"Up to you," she said with a shrug. "Maybe you'd rather stay innocent like Leena here, keep your expectations low enough for the guys to accomplish."

I turned to Mishail for support, and my eyes widened

when I realized Mishail's look was pensive, as if she was actually trying to decide whose side she was on.

"*Mishy?*" I said, heart beating loudly.

"I was just thinking," Mishail said, descending from her mysterious mountain of rainbows, "that we should have a party at Daria's house."

9

TAAHUD

I sat on the bed, watching Mishail as she knelt on the windowsill and placed her cheek against the wood. Her beige-and-coral frock was of delicate lace. Like the window, it was a kind of lattice that gave the illusion that you could see skin through it.

Absolutely scandalous, and Mishail knew it, because she said with glee, "There will be *boys* at the party."

My stomach dropped. I wanted to say, *You didn't tell me that before,* but I caught the words before I ended up sounding like Bilquis. I was annoyed with Mishail for enough other reasons. She hadn't defended me when Daria said I was innocent, making it sound like an insult. In fact, she and Daria were often called away together for debate preparations, so I saw very little of her these days. There wasn't even time to pick a fight.

"Mishy," I began.

"Don't worry. I won't leave your side. *Please?* It's just one night."

I sighed. I didn't know why I believed Mishail every single time, why all she had to say was *please* and all good sense left the building. *It's just talking on the phone with a boy, no big deal. He's very decent, nothing's happened, I promise. It's just to pass the time, nothing serious.*

"I know. I'm here, aren't I? I just don't think this is a good idea."

It was nearly November. It was a long time to have just been *talking* to boys on the phone. They had to have met or tried to meet. But it was illegal, and *muttaween* often raided the popular restaurants and cafés to break up dates. Surely Mishail wouldn't have been that stupid. I shook my head to clear my suspicions, but they snaked their way back in. The *muttaween* wouldn't raid the small, dark Pakistani restaurants of the slums in the southern part of the city, or the Ethiopian places in Manfouha that smelled of bleach. No, it was unthinkable that Mishail would have been stupid enough to meet with boys, total strangers, who would take her *there*. Disgusting.

And yet, if she'd *really* wanted it—

"When do you ever think having fun is a good idea?" Mishail asked, rolling her eyes. "Loosen up!"

I drew back, surprised at what sounded like irritation in her voice. Hadn't I always supported her, done whatever it took to satisfy her latest whim? Where was this coming from?

"Besides, Daria isn't going to be studying tonight."

My nostrils flared.

"I picked three possible dresses for you," Mishail went on, as if she hadn't just twisted the knife in my gut. "The color of your flesh for innocence, the color of your veins for power, or the color of blood if you're going for sexy."

I slapped my hands against my sides in despair. Mishail's fashion ideas always arrived with the suddenness of astrological proclamations.

"The color scheme is also true for roses," Mishail said, as if by way of explanation.

Being with Mishail wasn't a roller-coaster ride; it was like being swept up in a dust storm and dashed against all seven pillars of wisdom. It was addictive, and I couldn't get enough. And these days Mishail seemed to be rationing her time, three nights to me, two to Daria.

If I said anything to restrain Mishail, I knew the balance would flip against me.

"You picked innocence," I said, lightly touching the muddy-green dress in the middle that was supposed to signify power.

I meant, *I know you're keeping something from me.*

Mishail's head twitched, as if hearing something in the distance. She frowned. "Hurry up. My father's car just pulled in. He won't stay the night, but he likes to give us our daily scolding before he heads off to Number Two."

I smiled, because I knew Mishail expected me to whenever she referred to her father's second wife that way. I put on the dress that was supposed to make me seem powerful and stepped behind Mishail to see myself in the mirror. The dress had ribbing on the sides and front, leaving a hollow gap where my breasts would have gone if they existed. Mishail looked at me in the mirror and pulled out a padded bra with transparent straps from a drawer. She rapped the backs of her fingers against my shoulder, telling me to hurry up and put it on.

With a great clatter, Mishail emptied a large tray of makeup onto the counter and fished around for colors. She deftly rubbed shadows into her cheeks to make them more angular, and then held my jaw in her left hand and used her right to smudge a purplish lipstick onto my lips.

"How do I not get it on my teeth?" I asked.

"Kiss," Mishail said, grinning wickedly as she placed her thumb in my mouth. "Now it won't get on your teeth. Put on your *abaya*. I can hear him climbing the stairs."

There was a knock on the door, and Mishail put on her *abaya* before she opened it an inch, hiding her scandalous dress under the black cloak.

Frenetic whispers, and then the door closed. Mishail

sighed. "Can you wait outside? This is going to take a few minutes."

I veiled fully to cover my face and left the room. The minister pushed past me impatiently.

I leaned against the wall, hearing muffled whispers from the other side. I heard my name, Mishail explaining who it was. There was a clatter, as if the various articles of makeup were being thrown to the bathroom floor. The sound of glass shattering.

When the door opened again, the minister stormed out and for some reason looked directly at me. I was suddenly glad of the veil, which kept him from seeing me. The intensity on his face was terrifying. It reminded me that this was a man of tremendous power who could destroy me for the slightest sin. I hoped he couldn't see I was wearing lipstick.

He snarled, "Leena?"

I nodded mutely, surprised he even knew my name, never mind that he was speaking to me.

"Tell her to wait. The man's a fool. I did try to talk to him, but he won't sign."

I nodded again, wondering what he meant. The minister wiped a hand over his mouth. For a second he looked younger, less frightening, and I was reminded of the earlier days, before Mishail and I had to veil, when the minister and my father used to lounge on sofas, smoking apple-flavored *shisha* and arguing lazily.

The minister hadn't been a minister then. One night he'd been sitting with my father in the living room. My mother and Mishail's were veiled but not fully, relaxed in the presence of their husbands. It hadn't mattered then to keep up appearances of segregation, and Mishail and I had been fighting her brothers over a helium balloon.

My father had been saying something about nature finding a way, and he'd quoted some saying, probably the one about a river carving its own route.

"Don't say such things in front of them," my mother had said, her chin pointing at us.

"I wasn't talking about—" my father had replied, ending on a phrase I hadn't understood then and didn't remember now. This time all the other adults hushed him, and the boys let go of the balloon to listen to the conversation they weren't meant to hear. My father had laughed, said something else, and thrown an arm around Mishail's father to draw him in close.

They'd been friends once.

Now when the minister refused to move, I muttered, "Yes, sir."

The minister shook his head and walked off. I went into the room, expecting to find Mishail in tears or worse. Instead, she was leaning against the bathroom counter, curling her eyelashes, and studying her reflection in a shattered mirror.

"What happened?"

"Just a bad mood," Mishail said, her voice expression-less. She was applying skin-colored foundation onto the bruises forming on her arms. "Something about work. It's fine. I'm used to it. Don't worry. He didn't find out about the party."

I picked up the fallen pieces of lipstick and eyeliner. My hands were shaking with fear and fury. How could he treat us like this? How dare he leave bruises on my best friend that I could do nothing about? And how was Mishail so calm about it all?

"The maid will take care of it. And my mother's going to spend the rest of the evening sulking with her TV show."

I pulled Mishail into a hug and kissed her hair. Mishail held me close until my pulse slowed down, and then she let me go.

"My grandmother used to say," Mishail said, "women's hearts are like sand dunes. Everyone is welcome, but no one can leave footprints."

She smiled, meeting my eyes in the mirror. For a moment she looked wiser than any *imam*, looked like the amazing woman I hoped to be someday. Then she wiped off the dull-pink lipstick she had on, replacing it with a defiant cherry-red.

You chase the storm and I chase you, I thought, giddy as we raced downstairs to the waiting car.

A variety of emotions played across Mishail's features. Mouth determined but trembling slightly. Eyes flitting everywhere nervously, settling on mine every once in a while.

Softly, they said, *I know you're afraid of this.*

Then they got wet. *I really want this.*

And then they held that look that was ours alone. *Nothing will touch us.*

I looked away first. My face was hot. I wanted to say, *And what about Daria?* But that wasn't fair. There were enough prisons in our lives that friendship shouldn't be another. If Mishail wanted the company of someone else, that was what freedom was about, wasn't it? Besides, Mishail was always going to go places, move in more powerful circles. It had been only a matter of time before she outgrew my world. I had always been Number Two.

I blinked away the tears and forced my breathing back under control.

Daria's father was away on business again, and he had taken his wife with him, leaving Daria in the care of an eighteen-year-old cousin who was only too glad to let her throw a party while he played football with his friends. Mishail's driver pulled into the walled ARAMCO campus and rolled down his window to speak to the military officer guarding it.

As soon as the car was through the campus gate, Mishail threw off her *abaya* while I looked on in surprise. The houses inside the campus were small bungalows, barely separated from one another by hedges and rosebushes, with no walls in between. Nothing at all like the isolated, lonely villas of the rest of Riyadh. Neighbors could look into one another's houses through windows without bars or contact paper covering them. There were even parks where children played on swings and monkey bars. It took a moment for me to comprehend that I wasn't just seeing little kids. Boys and girls my own age were in the park. Together. They weren't doing anything sinful, either, just playing and talking.

A group of women jogged down the pavement in conversation, some wearing loose cotton full-sleeved shirts and track pants and a *hijab*, others in T-shirts and shorts, their ponytails bouncing from side to side.

I felt a knot in my throat at Mishail's lack of surprise.

"Have you been here before?"

"Just once or twice," Mishail said. But her voice was too high, and I looked away. I wondered if it wasn't Daria who had stolen Mishail's heart but this place and what it promised, and I didn't know whether that made me feel better or worse. I had a strange urge to shut my eyes to this so I wouldn't want to stay in this paradise forever, and the growing knot in my throat made me want to find something wrong, something *worse* about Daria's life that would make my own life bearable. And that, in turn, made me feel like the worst human on the face of the earth. So what if my best friend was finally, *finally*, getting to live her life? Given what Mishail had to deal with at home, she deserved this.

Inside the Abulkhair home, Daria sat on a high

four-poster bed with silver satin sheets, clutching an embroidered silk pillow. Girls gathered around her, dull as wallpaper, all the better for Daria to shine in contrast as empress of her court. Daria wore a bloodred gown that hung off one shoulder by a thin silver strap. The other shoulder was completely bare, the light shining on it as if it were polished porcelain.

A demon sat on one of my shoulders and said that Daria looked cheap, that respectable women did not dress like this. Another demon sat on the other shoulder and ached to look like her, a beautiful and confident woman who knew her own heart and mind.

"*Finally!*" Daria said, standing on her bed and jumping off to give Mishail a hug. "I thought you'd never get here. Now we can really start the party."

Mishail glowed at the attention. It was one of the things I loved most about her. Mishail was the most popular girl in school, but she was constantly surprised at being liked.

"Answer the question, Dee!" cried a young girl with a heart-shaped face, whom I recognized as an unveiled Zainab. "You can't leave us like this!"

"I'm not going to tell you," Daria said, swatting away Zainab's hand with a smile that showed off her dimples. "Well, I'm not going to tell you until you confess something first. How are things going with you and Mansoor?"

Zainab put the edge of her scarf in her mouth and bit

it shyly. "Mahmoud. But promise you won't tell anyone? That goes for everyone here." But she continued without waiting for the promise. "You were right, Dee. After I met Mahmoud, I realized there is nothing sexier than a real man, a serious one."

"Wow, madam," Mishail said, stiffening. "One month of engagement and you suddenly know everything about men, huh?"

"It really only takes one night," Daria said, winking, and the girls gasped and gave her high fives.

"Have you really sampled the merchandise?" asked Zainab, eyes darker than dates.

"Nah," Daria said, but the energy in the room crackled anyway. "I know my limits. I've never gone all the way. Just had a little snack, not the full dinner."

The older girls in the circle laughed loudly and gave Daria hugs. Unsure how to feel about it, I glanced at Mishail, surprised at the naked jealousy I saw on her face.

"Let's dance!" Daria declared, marching out to the living room, linking her arm through Mishail's as if claiming a consort. I bristled. Mishail didn't like being pushed around. Didn't Daria know that?

Once in the living room, Daria turned on a sound system that seemed to have speakers in all corners. All the American favorites forbidden to us, Lady Gaga and Taylor Swift and Beyoncé, streamed through uncensored and with a clarity I had never heard because we could only get pirated music shipped to us, years out of date and hidden inside the luggage of innocent-looking and elderly relatives.

My heart raced. I *wanted* to dance, wanted to be a part of this group, wanted to be at Mishail's side at the center of the makeshift dance floor, but I couldn't make my legs move. How did Mishail do it? The slow sashays of her hips ended with mischievous jerks, and she dragged her teeth across her lips with an averted gaze before sliding her fingers over her cheeks in a caress that left her skin the color of scorched sand dunes.

It was Daria, though, who took that place. Daria who headed for Mishail's side, who ran her fingers along Mishail's arms and up her sides without the slightest hesitation. Daria who spun Mishail out and pulled her back into an embrace, who put her hands on Mishail's head and drew her in until their foreheads touched.

I stood in the corner, cheeks burning. The only person I hated more than Daria in that moment was Mishail. She'd *promised* she wouldn't leave my side.

Did you really expect her to stand in a corner with you all night? asked a bitter voice in my head. I wondered where it had come from.

"And that's how they do it in New York!" Daria said as the song ended, laughing and taking a bow as the girls applauded, slack-jawed. "Come on up, and I'll teach you."

As each song played, Mishail slipped into every girl's

waiting arms willingly but would never let herself be held too long by anyone but Daria, who always swooped in for the best songs and claimed her place.

Everyone is welcome, but no one can leave footprints. Is that what you're doing, Mishy?

Suddenly, I realized someone was looking at me. I felt the weight of the attention before I even turned to see who it was. A boy stood at the curtained doorway, leaning against it with his arms crossed, watching the dance with an aloof and yet fond look in his eyes. From time to time he looked at me, and then his eyes had a question in them, as if he recognized me but couldn't place me.

Daria's cousin, I realized, seeing the resemblance. And another thing became blindingly obvious now. Mishail looked everywhere *except* at him, even though he was right *there*. Finally, I saw what I should have seen a long time ago. They were dancing to attract his attention. Mishail allowed herself to be held in Daria's arms, letting her eyes close in surrender. Daria's eyes met his boldly, as if inviting him over.

I narrowed my eyes at the boy. He was older, but not by much. Eighteen, Mishail had said. He was as handsome as Daria was beautiful, dark and hollow eyes in a serious, brooding face. His mouth was soft, and it was said that such men were of the weak type who let themselves be led by their mothers or their tribe. Sometimes I thought it was just a way we made ourselves feel better when we argued about why our favorite Egyptian actors who we fantasized about would make bad husbands.

Tariq would be the worse husband, I'd say to Mishail. *He has no personality in his face, soft chin and round cheeks like a sack of flour.*

Flour can be molded into shape, Mishail would say. *Which is what you want in a husband. But Farouq is an Aries, and that's not going to change. Irrational, stubborn, impulsive, always picking a fight and butting heads . . . that's fun for flirting, but not for marriage.*

I wondered how I could miss Mishail so much when she was standing in the same room.

To my surprise, the boy who had been looking at me smiled broadly and waved me over.

For a full minute I stood still and did the *who, me?* routine, shook my head, turned away, turned back, finally gave up, and inched over with all the suspicion of a street cat.

"What?" I asked as impolitely as I could to keep him from "getting any ideas." Daria and Mishail could make fools of themselves in front of him. I wasn't going to.

"You're her, aren't you?" he said unhelpfully. "Hadi Mutazil's daughter? Mishail's friend?"

"Best friend," I corrected him. "Who are you?"

"Ahmed. Daria's cousin. I've heard so much about you."

I relaxed, just a little. I still wasn't happy that this boy knew Mishail, that he was watching her as if he had the right, that Mishail knew him enough to have spoken to him about my father.

To my surprise, the boy bent down to whisper in my ear, coming so close that I shivered at the feeling of his breath against my face.

"We're all still with him, you know. We take courage in his strength."

What?

"Can we talk?" Ahmed said, jerking his head out of the room.

I hesitated. I turned to see Mishail and Daria glaring at me. How dare Mishail look so betrayed when she'd been the one to lie first, for *weeks*, keeping it secret that she'd had something going on with this guy?

"Sure," I said, reckless with anger but smiling brightly so he wouldn't see. I hadn't perfected Mishail's mask, but I knew when to use it. "Let's go somewhere quiet."

I let Ahmed lead me out into the courtyard, where date palms and golden streetlamps lined a broad pavement meant for campus residents to walk. I shivered, surprised at the feeling of cold air against my bare forearms and legs, suddenly hyperaware of being outdoors without an *abaya* and in the company of a non-*mahram* man. I'd never done this before, walked alongside a strange boy, and I felt an unnatural electricity at the closeness.

True, we were safe from arrest because we were within the ARAMCO campus, but we were still doing something dangerous. He walked so close to me that I could feel the warmth radiating from his skin. My pulse rose with guilty anticipation.

"My friends and I used to go to your father's *shillahs*," Ahmed said abruptly. "He'd text us the location, some apartment he'd rented on the outskirts of the city, a warehouse, a portable cabin somewhere. Sometimes we'd just meet in the open desert. We'd drop everything. Men who used to be religious but wanted something different. Young boys who were dropping out of school to drink *sid* and smoke drugs and wanted to turn their lives around. There were other movements, other *shillahs*. But they weren't the same. We didn't just admire Hadi. We *loved* him. He made us believe we could change the world."

I nodded, wondering why he was telling me this. He seemed desperate to get the words out, so I stayed quiet, knowing he'd eventually get to his point.

"You probably don't remember this," Ahmed said, "but we've met before. You were only a kid, so your father brought you along. It was a youth rally in the base—"

"I remember it," I said quietly. I couldn't bear it if he were to tell the story. It was bad enough that I remembered. I'd gone with my father after kicking up the usual tantrum over being left at home with my "boring" mother. (These days I'd take a *boring* parent over an *imprisoned* one.) This rally was in the basement of an office building. A janitor let us into a room of young men sitting on plastic chairs and debating whether reform would have any effect or if the extremists had the right answer and violence was the only way. I hadn't understood the debate, but I'd felt the reverberation of it, the heat and frustration of men who wanted very badly to do *something*, like flies trapped in a dirty bottle. I had turned around a second before I saw the terrible thing I'd somehow known was about to happen: a young man drawing his knife out and holding it to my father's neck.

"This is what they're doing to us!" the man cried, his eyes wet and fever-red. "Knives on all sides. Move an inch and they'll skin you alive, sew you up and skin you again, and tie your family to a car bumper and drag them by their ankles into the Rub Al-Khali. I've *seen* it, and you want us to be *patient*? You want us to say *Insh'allah* and wait for God to fix things?"

I had stood up and walked over, eyes fixed on my father's face. His eyes had met mine with perfect calm, and his voice when he spoke to his attacker was as affectionate as if he were speaking to me alone.

"Patience isn't weakness," he'd said. "There are things to be feared more than death. You're angry and impatient because you think things will change while you're alive. They won't. But they might change after you die. They might change *because* you died."

Ahmed was swallowing, scratching his head nervously. "Do you remember what he said? How calm he was?"

I nodded. We were walking side by side along the pavement as if we were old friends, as if the simple sharing of a childhood memory, even a violent one, was enough to make us relax around each other.

"He's my hero, Leena. I just had to say it. He opened my eyes. I've seen so much since then, things you'd never understand. Bootlickers like my father who take their *baksheesh* and let it stuff their mouths. Piece of shit—no, I won't apologize for calling them that—piece of shit men who just say *Insh'allah* because it's more convenient than doing anything. But Hadi Mutazil will never sign the *taahud*. He'll never give up."

I drew in a sharp breath. The autumn air sliced into my lungs and made me cough. I'd guessed that my father, like all political activists, would someday be given the *taahud*, a chance to confess to political crimes, recognize the king's generosity and forgiveness, and promise obedience in exchange for release.

It just hadn't occurred to me that he wouldn't sign.

That he wouldn't *want* to return to the family he'd supposedly been fighting for all along.

"And neither will we," Ahmed said. "There are so many of us now. We text one another about meeting places because e-mail is monitored. We'd die for him. I wish you could see it."

Still, I didn't speak. It wasn't pride but rage that was coursing through me, anger that seemed sudden but also inevitable, as if it had been building for years. My father wasn't coming home. Not because he couldn't, but because it would injure his pride to surrender to the government. I felt like such a fool for my patience. For trusting him. For trusting Mishail.

The reality was that sometimes even your mother and father couldn't take care of you because they were too busy proving some point or fighting each other. And stupidity was letting yourself be the doormat your loved ones walked on. In the worst moments of your life, you were always alone.

"As soon as I saw you, I knew I had to say something," Ahmed said. He seemed calmer now, as if he'd just confessed a crime of his own. "Your father changed my life. Other men will settle down, get regular jobs, and get as fat as their government salaries. They'll marry and they'll drive more slowly and they'll forget the desert they came from."

I stopped walking, my brain firing a torrent of warning signals so that I knew what he was going to confess even before the words came out of his mouth.

"I can't tell Mishail any of this. She's really sweet, but innocent. Not like us. You understand, don't you?"

I nodded, my heart skipping a beat at the way he called Mishail innocent.

I wasn't surprised at all when Ahmed said, "I kept asking Mishail when I could meet you, but she never arranged it."

I was only a little surprised at myself when I gave Ahmed my phone number and asked if I could join him sometime. If I could see what was so amazing about my father's world that he'd rather stay in prison than give it up and come home.

10

QAYAMAT

We couldn't talk in the car with the driver listening, but we'd never needed words. I could feel Mishail's anger, a cold fury that froze the air between us.

When we'd been silent for fifteen minutes, even the driver seemed to notice. He cast worried looks in the rearview mirror.

"So what were you and"—Mishail cleared her throat—"*Amina* talking about? You guys disappeared for so long we thought you got lost."

I shook my head, smiling. Mishail's curiosity always got the better of her. She couldn't wait until we were home to ask, but she hadn't bothered to mention her own interest in Ahmed or the details of her friendship with Daria, so what right had she to demand this?

"Football," I said, matching Mishail's coldness measure for measure.

Mishail glared.

"That campus gives you a false sense of security," Mishail said. "You think anything is allowed because you're inside those walls, but if something is happening, like a girl and a boy getting together, the neighbors find out and talk about it."

It was my turn to glare. I said, "Why do we pay the *mahabith* when we can just spy on one another for free?"

The car swerved slightly at the mention of the *mahabith*, the secret police, indicating that the driver had heard us. Mishail withdrew into silence, and I looked out the window at the empty lots that separated the high-rises of the northwest quadrant of the city. Whiteland, they called it, the rubble and dust that was too expensive to actually build on but sold for millions as it passed hands from prince to corrupt dealer to bureaucrat without ever being cultivated into anything real. Boys played football in some, drove around in circles in others like lazy moths.

I itched to have a real fight with Mishail, instead of this silly sideswiping. The car pulled into Mishail's driveway, and we got out, climbing the stairs in heavy, angry steps that echoed throughout the long corridors.

Mishail slammed open the door of her room, and I

slammed it shut. Mishail's mother moaned something in protest, but we ignored her, eager to let out the frustrations of the evening. I wondered when it had started, this thrumming underneath my skin that itched like a beast to be set free. I'd felt it more in the last two months, once the temperature had started to drop low enough for it to rain. There were days when the hail crashed against the covered-up windows, and I would lean out for a quick moment to catch the drops on my tongue and breathe in the dust, the scent leaving me frantic and confused, blood sloshing about my body and dragging against my edges at breakneck speed.

My pulse raced.

"You had no right to do that," Mishail said. "I invited you. You were there as my *guest*."

"What exactly did I do that I wasn't supposed to?"

"You embarrassed me. You made me look like a fool in front of everyone, behaving so indecently."

I took a step forward, backing Mishail into a corner. "You were doing a good enough job of embarrassing yourself. Tell me, what did I do that was so wrong? Go for a walk with a boy? I wasn't the one rolling around practically naked for his benefit."

Mishail blushed, her skin turning as coral as her dress. Her eyes filled.

I drew back to breathe. Mishail slipped past me and went into the bathroom, closing the door. I placed my arms against the window and looked out at the empty street through the slitted shutters. It felt as if the fight had been postponed, and I didn't know why I felt disappointed by that. I didn't want to make Mishail cry, not really, but I didn't have words to explain what I *did* want. I was still reeling from the sense of loss and betrayal that I'd felt in that moment when Mishail's eyes fluttered closed while she was in Daria's arms, when Daria presented her to Ahmed like an offering.

When Mishail came out of the bathroom, she was wearing her pajamas. She looked even younger without makeup, a child swimming in stupidly big pants that had hearts and flowers all over them. It made me want to laugh.

She said, with grim determination, "I haven't even told Daria this, but I think Ahmed is in love with me. He says he can't be in a relationship yet because he has to do something first, but I can tell when we talk that he's struggling against temptation."

I rolled my eyes as I went into the bathroom to get my makeup off. I felt sick.

"How do you think Daria will react when she finds out?" I couldn't resist saying. "Think she'll keep inviting you over when she realizes you stole the guy she wants? And are you sure he isn't lining up wives one and two at the same time?"

"He's not like other boys," Mishail said. "He's not tough

or mean, and he's not looking for random flirting like the idiots at Faisaliyah. Something happened to Ahmed when he was young. Something he won't talk about to anybody. I'm the only one to whom he admitted that, and even to me he wouldn't say what it was, just that he wasn't like other guys. He's dedicated his life to something far greater than the gold and girls that the others are after. He needs a gentle touch, and you—you can be kind of sharp. I'm just being honest, because I'm your friend and I don't mind it, but it's true."

I looked at Mishail's reflection in the mirror. Something there twisted my gut, a resentment in Mishail's tone that was coming out in the guise of friendly honesty but had been years in the making. It made me want to break my promise to Ahmed, to say with the same icy sweetness, *Oh yes, he told me all about it. But I promised I wouldn't tell you.*

Instead, I washed my face with cold water and closed the bathroom door. Hurt was pulsing through my body, a throbbing that made dark spots cloud my vision. I didn't *want* to be sharp, but when I was angry, words sometimes came out of my mouth like shattered glass. I knew I *should* be softer, I *should* endure as other women did, with quietness and grace. Didn't Mishail know that it was what I loved most about her?

I left the bathroom no calmer than when I went in. "I just want what's best for you," Mishail said. "I don't want you getting your heart broken. It's best to catch these things early. You're just not his type."

"How do you know that?" I asked through my teeth.

Mishail sighed. "Don't you think I can tell these things? There's a difference between a crush and real love. I know you're attracted to him. I could see that right away. How could you help it? You're so sheltered, of course you'd fall for the first guy you see. But that's not love."

"I'm *sheltered*?"

"When it comes to these things, yes, you're really innocent," Mishail said, as if she were at the edge of her patience. "When a guy really thinks a girl is sexy, he flirts from a distance. He doesn't just ask to talk to her seriously. The fact that Ahmed did that probably means he thinks of you as a sister."

I froze. The word *sister* came at me like a punch.

"That's not—" I began, intending to say it wasn't true. Instead, I finished with, "I don't even like him that way. We're just friends."

"Boys and girls can't be friends," Mishail said, her eyes full of sympathy. "It always turns into something else. Thoughts get polluted. Look, I just don't want you getting hurt."

"*You're* trying to protect *me*?" I asked, crossing my arms and huffing out a laugh. "Does it bother you that much that for once in our lives, someone actually paid more attention to *me* than to you?"

Mishail sighed. She took out her phone, shimmering in a sparkly pink case. She showed me the history of her messages to and from Ahmed.

Loved your dress tonight. So feminine!

Are you teasing me?

I don't tease. And you're such a great dancer!

Next time you should join us, if you dare. Or are you a traditional guy, who only dances with other guys even at his wedding?

Ha! Don't get me started.

My ears rang, a teakettle sound that silenced everything else. I knew I'd gone statue-still, that Mishail was watching my reaction.

I burst into tears.

I was distantly aware of Mishail leaping off the bed to calm me down, and then we were in each other's arms saying we were sorry for the things we'd said. Mishail kept saying she didn't think I could *cry*, never mind have a crush, and all the while I was trembling with more anger and heartache than I thought I could bear. In just one night, I had fallen for Ahmed, and I knew now that he didn't see me that way. I'd learned that he and Mishail were at least flirting, even if they hadn't actually done anything. And if Daria found out, or worse yet, the minister, the pain I felt now would be nothing compared with what we would all have to endure.

Later, we were lying in bed, and I said, "This is *dangerous*, Mishy. It's not like the other stuff."

Mishail's fingers stroked my hair absently.

"I'm serious. This isn't a prank you can just recover from. It changes you. And if your father found out, there's no telling what he'd do."

"I've never understood," Mishail said, "where you got this separation between serious crimes and silly pranks. Before he married Number Two, my father once took me to his work, and I thought I could be some kind of spy, prove that the only thing she wanted was money, or find out some state secrets and blackmail him into breaking it off."

I turned to face Mishail, wondering where this was going, and more important, why Mishail had never told me this before. The arrival of the second wife had been a painful year for Mishail, but lately she'd only ever talked about the benefits: less scrutiny, a paid driver who didn't ask questions, peace and quiet a few nights a week.

"I saw a man who was clearly a *muttawa*, and he looked serious and nervous, as if he had some huge revelation to share with my father. He was clutching a report in his fingers as if it were made of gold leaf. My father read it, and then took the man into the special inner room for a private talk. Naturally, I read it. You know what it said?"

I shook my head, surprised when Mishail started shaking with laughter.

"It was a report on delinquency among youth. A list of statistics about what fifteen- to eighteen-year-olds were doing and how the trends showed steep social decline or something. Fifteen percent had worn T-shirts with the image of a pop star on them. Eighty-five percent had smoked a cigarette or used a curse word in the last six months."

Mishail placed one hand over her eyes, unable to continue she was laughing so hard. I reached for Mishail's other hand and squeezed it.

"That's when I knew," Mishail said, "that none of it mattered. That the world was a stupid joke and I was going to hell anyway, so I might as well do whatever I want and have fun. When the Day of Judgment comes, I know what I'll have to answer for, and it won't be for the things I've done. It'll be for all the things I want to do."

Her eyes fixed on mine with an intensity that had a hint of madness.

"I understand what you're saying," she continued. "I really do. What I feel for Ahmed is—it's not a crush. It's like I'm finally alive after being buried underground for sixteen years. If I don't hear from him for a few hours, I go crazy. I text him every twenty minutes, and I know that's not right, but I can't stop. We tell each other every stupid thing that happens in the day. When we touch, even for a second, it's like—" She made an explosive *whoosh* sound. "I can't explain it. You wouldn't understand if you haven't felt it. And despite all that, he makes me a better Muslim, because he believes that the true connection between people isn't physical, it's a bond of the soul."

I turned away from Mishail, letting hot tears slide into the pillow. I wanted to tell her, *I do understand, Mishy. How it feels to want something so much you might end up setting yourself and the world on fire to get it.*

"I know it's dangerous," Mishail said. "Everything we want is forbidden or dangerous. I just don't care."

11

WISKHA

I stirred the liquids in the beaker with a glass rod. The oil formed large bubbles over the water that congealed until they formed a sort of chandelier over the water below. Our chemistry teacher went on about miscible and immiscible liquids as if it were supposed to be an earth-shattering surprise that oil and water did not mix.

Do you remember where we live? I thought, still stirring idly. My mind flew to the scent of gasoline that permeated the city streets, how on rainy days Mishail and I would chase each other around her courtyard looking for oil stains that shifted in the sunlight. Why couldn't we stay those children forever, whose greatest worry was whether we'd be allowed to eat two Rico bars that day instead of one? Why did we have to deal with scholarships and marriage and parents who wouldn't come home from prison? Why did Mishail have to go and fall in love with a rebel?

Mishail was standing next to me in the chemistry lab, but her attention was focused entirely on Daria, her boundless happiness rising off her in sickening bursts. The two of them were being incredibly annoying, speaking in glances and dissolving into giggles. I scowled, knowing they were that friendly only because Mishail hadn't yet told Daria about her growing relationship with Ahmed. I was sure that whenever that news came out, Daria would cut her down with even less mercy than she'd shown Bilquis.

I used the dropper to add two drops of blue food coloring to the mixture. Chemistry was required to get into petrochemical engineering, and, realistically, what else were you going to do in this country, but the kinds of experiments girls were permitted to do were too small to teach us anything. Still, it was better than medicine, where biology textbooks were considered too obscene for women, so we had to simply imagine what was under the black censorship ink. For all I knew, the male body had more in common with the shrimp that came in from Dammam than the female body.

It was all very well for Mishail to swoon over the epic story of it all: Minister's daughter and rebel engaging in a star-crossed romance under the very nose of the man responsible for protecting the virtue of women all over the country. But what about afterward? The trouble with Mishail was that she trusted people too much, didn't think ahead, and didn't believe anyone would use her secrets against her or her family. How could she rush toward boys and sex when she knew how it could—*would*—end: in tears, pregnancy, or death?

Mishail bit her lower lip. My ears grew hot. What if it was too late? There was already something older, less innocent, about Mishail. In the last two weeks, she'd gone from girl to woman, held herself up straighter, knew when people were looking at her, and turned to give them a camera-ready smile.

Mishail raised her hand to go to the bathroom. I was about to follow her, but Daria caught my wrist. I was too surprised not to stay back and hear what she had to say.

"I know you think I stole your best friend," Daria said when Mishail was gone. I drew my hand back, stung that she had seen through me so easily.

"Mishail's not a purse to be stolen," I said. "She chooses her friends."

"Of course, sorry," Daria said. Her tone was so gentle that I relaxed a little. "Look, at the end of the day, we both love her and want what's best for her. Don't you agree?"

I nodded reluctantly.

"It's why I wanted to talk to you. I'm really worried about her. Something has her completely distracted from the debate."

I held my breath and practiced making my face as neutral as possible.

"Look, if you can't tell me what it is, do you at least know how to help her?" Daria asked, looking flustered. "That's all I want. I know you and I are very different, but you know her best. If she's in trouble, you're the only one who can help her, not me."

I smiled, feeling for the first time that I didn't have to hate Daria with every cell in my body.

"What can I do?"

"She won't tell me," Daria said, "but I think I know what it is. I think it's my cousin, Ahmed. I think he and Mishail are—you know."

I frowned, wondering if this was a trap, if Daria was trying to find out the truth by getting me to admit to Mishail's secret.

"I don't mind if they are," Daria said quickly. "I'm not one to judge. You know I've had experience, so I don't think it's *zina*. It's just that the debate is really important. To both of us. It's our future, and I don't want Mishail to throw it away. That's what matters to me."

"Is Mishy missing practice sessions?"

"No, but she has some special plans for this weekend that she wouldn't tell me about."

I felt a prick of hurt as I realized that Mishail had not mentioned a word about it to me, either. "I think the plan is to—" And Daria leaned in to whisper just one word: *120*. As in, what we'd read on page 120 of that book.

My blood froze. A few moments passed, so slowly and thickly I wondered if the oil in our beakers had permeated the atmosphere. I felt that a breath out of place would ignite the very air.

"Some girls can do this kind of thing and it doesn't touch them," Daria said. "One guy yesterday, one guy today, and then ace a test tomorrow. But doing *that* can turn even the strongest girls into a puddle. And Mishail . . ."

She trailed off. I nodded, feeling very sluggish. Mishail entered the classroom, and Daria flew back to her own experiment.

"Hey, Mishy," I asked after what felt like an eternity had passed. "What are your plans for the weekend?"

Mishail frowned in surprise.

"Why?"

"Never mind," I said, hurt by her refusal to tell me.

"I'm going to a friend's house," she said slowly. Her eyes were fixed on mine, and I couldn't tell if she was hoping I would understand or hoping I wouldn't. "Her parents are away for the weekend."

"Does this *friend* have a name?"

Mishail rolled her eyes, running her finger through the open flame of the Bunsen burner absently.

"Stop chatting back there and work on your lab report!" the chemistry teacher said, startling us.

"I'll be back," I said, muttering something about the bathroom but just needing to get out of the classroom and breathe. My face was on fire. What the hell was Ahmed thinking, getting so deeply involved with the minister's daughter? And were he and Mishail really—I couldn't even finish the thought.

The bell rang, and I was about to go back inside when Daria slipped out to find me. She grabbed my arm and led me to a bathroom stall.

"So?" she asked. "Did you find out anything?"

I nodded, and then hastily shook my head. "Only guesses."

"But she and Ahmed are serious, right?" Daria asked. Her voice had a panicked edge. I didn't trust myself to speak. "You know we have to do something before it's too late."

"We should talk to Maryam Madam," I said.

"Are you insane? We'll all be expelled!"

"No, she'll find a quiet way to stop it. She won't let scandal fall on the minister's name. She's always made sure we don't go too far."

Daria drew back, considering what I'd said. Her eyes were narrowed in concentration. Finally, her face brightened.

"You're right," she said, squeezing my hands. "You're absolutely right. You know what's best for Mishail. Are you going to the headmistress's office now?"

"I probably should, shouldn't I?"

"You're a really good friend," she said. "I know you don't like me very much, and this debate thing—"

"No, it doesn't matter," I said, and meant it. No stupid

debate or scholarship could possibly compare to protecting Mishail. This Ahmed thing had gone too far. If I had felt so miserable after having known Ahmed for a few hours, Mishail wouldn't survive it if he broke her heart. And he would. He would go to jail, or the minister would kill him, or he'd go off to university. That was what men did, went off to follow their personal *jihads* and assumed that the virgins they got in paradise would make up for all the women's hearts they'd broken down here.

I left the bathroom stall and walked straight to the headmistress's office. I hesitated before knocking on the door. What I was about to do terrified me. I didn't think I could even get the words out.

Thoughts get polluted, I remembered with a shudder. *Oh, Mishy.*

"Come in."

The headmistress had on square, rimless glasses that made her eyes look bigger than they were. Across from her desk, Naseema Madam sat, straight-backed, hands in her lap as if she were being punished.

"Could I speak with you alone?"

Maryam Madam sighed.

"Leena, darling, anything you have to tell me you should feel free to tell Naseema as well. We make all decisions together. She's as much headmistress as I am."

I frowned, catching sight of Naseema Madam's surprised smile. I still didn't like her very much, but I now saw what Maryam Madam was doing, putting out a little milk every chance she got to win over a cat that had never known kindness.

"Leena, does this concern Daria and Mishail?" My expression must have spoken for me, because Maryam Madam removed her glasses and said, "Close the door."

"You might think we don't see, but we do," Naseema Madam said. "We know our girls. We see the cliques and the *shillahs*, and we know who's headed for trouble."

"I think we have some idea of what's on your mind," Maryam Madam said. "Take a seat."

"I don't want to get anyone in trouble," I said, stalling for time to think. It was one thing to tell Maryam Madam, who might punish us but would protect us from the *muttaween*. I wasn't so sure about Naseema Madam, who was about as expressive as a used chalkboard.

"Leena, one girl spent the night in a boy's room at KAUST and there were nationwide *riots*. I know you're trying to keep Mishail from trouble, but I need you to think about everyone else. About the whole school."

"There was a party two weekends ago. At Daria's house."

Maryam Madam drew herself up. Naseema Madam said nothing, but her dark eyes fixed on me angrily. I could tell she was embarrassed that one of her own had broken a rule.

"Thank you, Leena," Maryam Madam said. "I know it's

fashionable to have parties, but if the *muttaween* were to raid it, there's no telling—"

"Daria lives in the ARAMCO campus. No *muttaween*."

The headmistress frowned. I felt a burst of affection for her. If there was ever any doubt that the headmistress was on our side, that she would let the little battles go, this was it. Her frown practically said, *If you're not going to get caught, why is this a problem?*

"Leena, was this a mixed party?" Naseema Madam asked.

I nodded hesitantly.

Naseema Madam leaned forward, eyes suddenly blazing. She asked, "Leena, do you know what slander is?"

"It is to say something about a person that they would not like. To cast suspicion."

"And what is the punishment if what you say is not proved?"

I swallowed. "Death."

Even if I hadn't actually known the answer, it was a pretty fair guess for any crime. How often had Mishail and I breezed through law tests simply checking off the harshest penalty on every multiple choice? *Death, death, death,* following us around through our daily activities like a bratty little sister.

"So if you were at Daria's party, then why are you bothered that there were boys there? You were part of the sin, were you not?"

I glared at Naseema Madam. Here I was trying to help and she was interrogating me before I could get a sentence together, trying to make this my fault as well, not just Daria's.

"I'm not here about the party. I'm here because I'm worried about what might happen next. To Mishail. Daria can take care of herself."

Maryam Madam sat up straight in her chair.

"Has Mishail been acting sinfully?" Naseema Madam asked. I scowled.

"She's giving us time to prevent the sin," Maryam Madam said. "Can't you see she doesn't want to do this?"

"Why *are* you doing this, Leena? Is it because of the internship? You think if Mishail's reputation is ruined, you'll be the replacement?"

"*What? No!*"

"It's not like that," Maryam Madam said in my defense. "Leena would protect Mishail with her life."

"Then what?" Naseema Madam asked. "Why are you here?"

This was it. I had to either say something or walk away. I closed my eyes and tried to think of any other way out. I knew Mishail wouldn't listen to me or see sense. If anything, she'd probably go even further if I tried to stop her. She would think I was acting out of jealousy, trying to keep her from having Ahmed because he didn't want me.

I said through gritted teeth, "I don't know for sure, but I believe Mishail is involved with a boy. I think it's serious."

The door burst open. I had been so focused on the two headmistresses, and so nervous about what I was saying, that I hadn't realized someone had been listening in. I turned in horror to see Mishail flying at me, her face wild with rage. Behind her, Daria had a triumphant smile on her face.

"*Wiskha!*" Mishail hissed, grabbing my hair and smashing my head into the wall.

She couldn't have said anything worse. It meant dirty, deviant, corrupt. The word stung me to my soul.

"What's going on?" Naseema Madam asked, standing up to get away from Mishail.

"I *hate* you!" Mishail screamed. "*I hate you!* How could you do this to me? How could you tell them? I *trusted* you. I'll kill you. After *everything* we've done? You're *nothing* to me, you hear? *Nothing!*"

Mishail spat on my face. I tensed against it but said nothing. I couldn't feel my legs. Was this really happening? Was this really my Mishail saying these horrible things?

"Mishail," the headmistress said. She reached forward and grabbed Mishail by the waist, struggling to pull her off me. I sat dazedly on the floor. My face burned where Mishail had scratched me.

"To tell her about the party was one thing, but you told her about *Ahmed*? Daria always warned me you'd betray me for the stupid internship, but I didn't believe her."

"Mishail, *be quiet*," Maryam Madam said, but Mishail shook her head, struggling against her grasp.

"I was trying to protect you," I said, but Mishail wasn't listening. My head was still spinning, trying to make sense of what had just happened. Daria had planned this. She had played us against each other, and I had just betrayed my best friend's deepest secret. A surge of fear and pain pulsed through me, almost doubling me over.

Daria had wanted to separate me and Mishail, but why? She was outside the door, out of the headmistresses' view, but before she disappeared, for a moment I saw the gleeful hatred on her face when she looked at Mishail.

Realization finally struck. This hadn't been about the debate at all. This wasn't even about *me*. This was about Ahmed choosing Mishail. So Daria was willing to destroy Mishail's future over Ahmed. I didn't understand it at all.

"Who's Ahmed?" Naseema Madam asked.

Maryam Madam pinched her temples, as she always did when she was tired.

"Mishail, *are* you involved with a boy?" she asked, her voice trembling with anxiety.

Mishail burst into tears, screaming unintelligible curses at me. But there must have been something about her expression that the older women knew how to read, because Naseema Madam slumped against the wall. The headmistress's hands shook, and she held the desk for support as she sat down.

"*Fi aman Allah*," Maryam Madam said, her face pale and gray. *May God protect us.*

Naseema Madam said, "We have to do something. Call Mishail's parents, maybe—"

"*No!*" Mishail screamed. "Don't tell them. I'll do anything. My father will kill me. *Please*, don't tell them!"

I wondered what was happening to me. I could hear everything the others said, but the words sounded as if they were coming from far away, and I couldn't bring myself to speak. I was there and yet not, in a world where Mishail had never said the words that had cut me loose from life as I knew it, a world where I watched the life drain out of Daria's eyes with something that felt like joy. I forced myself to pay attention.

"It's only going to get worse," Naseema Madam said to Maryam Madam. "Maybe we should just give up. It's not worth it. If anything goes wrong, they'll shut down the school. And that's the best-case. Remember what happened to Zorah?"

There were many Zorahs in the world, but there was ever only one in our minds. A fifteen-year-old from Buraydah who had celebrated Valentine's Day by sending a love letter to a boy and was stoned to death in punishment. I shuddered. I could hardly bear to look at Mishail right now, but even she trembled at that name.

"But if we can save even one . . . ," Maryam Madam said, her eyes like steel. She didn't finish her sentence. Her voice sounded shredded, as if she was about to cry.

Naseema Madam looked at her for a long time and then nodded. She said, "Girls, go back to class. We'll let you know when we've made a decision."

12

WIRAN

The decisions were made in minutes and put into place so quickly that by the weekend, Aisha was talking about debate prep as if she'd been doing it for weeks. She had replaced Mishail, who was deemed to be too much of a risk, and who had at any rate been suspended for two weeks. Aisha's father was a doctor at King Fahd Hospital, so nobody could claim that Aisha was anything other than a good girl, who would be a good influence on Daria.

I heard through the grapevine that someone had suggested very delicately to Mrs. Quraysh that some mother-daughter time might be appropriate. Mishail wasn't answering my calls, and I wasn't talking to Daria, and the headmistresses told me with matching sad faces that they wished my unfortunate situation were different.

"You understand, don't you?" Maryam Madam asked. "I promise we'll find something that's right for you. Trust me, just a little longer."

"I don't care about the internship," I said angrily. "I don't care about anything anymore. I don't even care if Mishail's father does kill her. I'm going to tell him what she and Daria were doing, just so they get what they deserve."

Naseema Madam flinched. I hated her for choosing Aisha over me for the debate. Aisha could barely string together the five fundamental pillars of Islam, and she was going to get a chance to work with our country's leaders?

"You don't mean that," the headmistress said. "Leena, I know what's happened to you, what's still happening; I know it's unfair. But what I've always been proud of is the way you try to save others from being treated unfairly, instead of trying to punish those who treat *you* unfairly. That's what I've come to expect from you. You won't disappoint me, will you?"

I blinked away tears. I hated Maryam Madam for not getting angry, for trying to calm me down when what I really wanted was for her to give me an excuse to join the *tufshan*, to accept that I had no future and would burn the world down. What was the use of trying to be a good girl here? Of preserving what was left of a reputation that looked like the underwear of a street urchin from Naseem while my father was in prison and didn't care what happened to me? I was never going to be a lawyer. I wasn't even going to get into university. So, that weekend, I agreed to join Ahmed after all. Why not?

At the party, Ahmed had told me to sleep next to my phone, and he'd finally called at around two on Wednesday morning. Mishail was right about one thing. His voice was a drug. Even knowing that he didn't see me that way didn't help. I'd said something in my half-asleep state that he thought was funny, and his laughter made me shiver. His parents were out of town over the weekend, my mother was busy catering some multiday wedding, and Mishail was being forcibly sent to the *hammam* for her mother-daughter spa intervention. We were free.

Ahmed picked me up in a white Toyota Camry. It was old and beaten-up, and curses were rubbed into the dust on the windows, so I knew the car couldn't possibly be his.

"My license plate can be traced," Ahmed said, sensing my unasked question. "This is safer."

I clutched my cold and sweaty hands in my lap to keep them from shaking. I knew that boys stole cars all the time here and that the Camry in particular was the most stolen car in the country, if not the world. But I'd always thought it was the work of thugs in the lower-income district. But, of course, I'd never known any boys, so I really had no way to judge who was or wasn't a thug. For all I knew, all boys were thugs.

"We'll take it back when we're done. Don't worry. And there's no damage. My friend Mohammed works at the dealership, so he has master keys. Cars are nothing here."

I wrapped the checkered headdress more tightly around my face. I was wearing my father's thin white *thobe*. For some reason, as the car started, I felt that all my years of dressing up as a man were practice for this moment. Surveillance cameras were on every street corner, and *muttaween* in their vans pulled up alongside us to inspect the car's inhabitants, but none of them, even the ones who stared at me for the entire red light, stopped us. Ahmed headed south, past the reach of the police and toward the sprawling suburban districts on the outskirts of the city, where new developments were perpetually expanding into the desert. Sometimes there were construction sites, but more often than not there were simply perfect, freshly laid roads and empty lots. Under Riyadh's signature golden streetlamps, swarms of locusts cast fluttering shadows on the road as if it were some kind of disco.

The city was starting to hunker down for the upcoming month of Ramadan. When the month of purity and fasting happened to fall in the winter, Riyadh had a buzzing energy to it that it didn't have in the hot summer months, when people mostly lay down indoors and prayed for the horribleness to end.

There was a group of boys in the distance. Ahmed slowed down the car, as if suddenly feeling hesitant.

"You think they'll be able to tell?" I asked.

"Not if you don't talk much."

"So what is it?"

My heart raced. What was I thinking? I was alone with a boy I barely knew, whom I was trusting simply because he'd known my father. And even if *he* could be trusted, there was a battalion of men ahead, more than I'd ever seen together in one place.

"What is it?" I asked again.

"If anyone asks, say that you belong to me and you'll be safe."

"What does that mean, I belong to you? And safe from what?"

Ahmed tapped his fingers on the steering wheel as if pondering a speech, and I pondered opening the door and jumping out while the car was moving. Coming here was a stupid idea.

"Not like that," Ahmed said hurriedly. "It's nothing. Don't worry. I won't let anything happen to you."

That wasn't very practical or reassuring, but my stupid heart leaped anyway. I peered into the distance to see whether I could at least outrun the group. As if that were any kind of a plan, running back home in the middle of the night. Why had I come? I wanted to know these people who loved my father. I wanted to understand—

Nonsense, said a bitter voice in my head. *You wanted to come close to the fire without getting burned. You wanted to show Mishail that you weren't some innocent who couldn't handle herself around boys. You wanted to impress her, make her jealous.*

I told that voice to shut up. If Mishail was done with me, I was done with her, too. This wasn't about her at all.

To my immense relief, nobody paid me any notice. The boys simply sat around on the trunks of their cars and shared their frustrations and their cigarettes, here in the open desert away from police and cameras. One of them had a father who beat him. Another had been expelled from school for writing blasphemous poetry. He kept reciting his favorite line, even though I was convinced I had heard it before.

Everything is forbidden, so we can do anything.

"And what about you? What brought you here?" one of them asked me. He'd had his eyes on me for a while, making me glad the headdress covered my face.

I looked at Ahmed to see if he'd shared some story that I'd have to play along with.

"Oh, I see how it is," the boy said, laughing. "The passive one becomes active."

His words made no sense to me, but something about the way he'd said it made me realize it was a crude joke. Ahmed rolled his eyes.

"Tell you what, *wiran*," the guy said, making a V with his fingers and pointing it at my eyes. "I'll do a little dance. For your eyes only."

He slid off the roof of the car he was sitting on and got inside, starting the engine.

"What's he doing? Why did he call me *wiran*?"

"Showing off," Ahmed said, ignoring my other question. "That's Coca-Cola."

I raised an eyebrow.

"It's his nickname because he looks like the bottle. And because his family got rich smuggling it into the country when it was banned."

Coca-Cola drove his old BMW (*also probably stolen*) down the road until his rear lights were a small and dusty pair of red eyes. Then the car turned around and headed toward us. Clearly, something important was about to happen, because the boys stopped gossiping and started to pay attention. Some of them stood up expectantly, gazing down the road.

We heard the car before we saw what was happening, the screeching tires sending up a puff of dust. The boys started clapping and screaming and yodeling. The BMW barreled toward us at highway speed, doing a figure eight that nearly grazed a dozen streetlamps before screeching to a halt ten feet in front of us.

I realized one of my hands was covering my mouth while the other was digging into Ahmed's arm. I let go of him quickly, embarrassed, wiping my hand as if to clean away the crime of having touched a boy.

Coca-Cola got out of the car and headed toward us. He made a lewd sound, and then reached down and turned his hand into a claw. I'd seen men do that in the park, on the bus, and even a few times on the street. Before I'd started dressing as a boy, one of them had reached for me and grabbed a breast for a quick grope when I went to the *bakhala* to buy milk, saying a cheerful *"shukran"* afterward as if thanking me for good service.

But this guy's hand was reaching down, way below my chest.

Ahmed stepped in front of me at the last minute, doubling over in pain when the hand made contact somewhere below his stomach. I blew out a breath in gratitude. I didn't think I could handle random guys touching me out here.

"Okay, okay," Coca-Cola said, putting his arms up in surrender. "But you have to admit I'm good. Not as good as Hadi, but who is? It's just a surprise that *you* would ever love anybody else."

I frowned in confusion. What could the guy possibly mean?

But soon the boys were engrossed in a conversation about how to expose a prince's son who had killed someone in a fight in Manfouha. The police had not arrested him, even though nearly six witnesses were on the street. We thought of ways to blackmail the killer into paying the required *diyyat*, or blood money, to the victim's family.

I wondered if there was really a difference between helping the innocent and punishing the guilty. I'd wanted to become a lawyer for the same reason as anybody else. A fire burned deep within me to help the people who deserved happiness find it. And sometimes, as now, that fire also burned to punish those who were undeserving who had found happiness anyway.

"This is really dangerous," I said to Ahmed.

"I know," Ahmed said. He swatted impatiently at a locust. He said in English, in a fake American accent, "It's a dirty job, but someone has to do it."

"But why this?" I gestured vaguely at the road to indicate the crazy driving.

"To remind ourselves of the few things that still make life worth living. But why don't you find out for yourself?" Ahmed asked, dangling keys over my head. I jumped up to grab them, grinning so hard my cheeks hurt.

We got into the Camry. The engine came to life with a hitching wheeze and then a roar, and I gripped the steering wheel as if it were an animal that might bolt. Being in the driver's seat was different from anything I'd ever experienced. Raw power flowed through my veins. My skin tingled, and goose bumps rose up on my arms.

"The road's a straight line, but you probably don't want to go too fast until you learn how to turn," Ahmed said. He reached over until he was practically sharing the seat with me and in the darkness used his hand to place my right foot on the brake. I could hardly breathe, completely disoriented by his grip on my ankle.

"And this," he said softly, as he moved my foot again, "is the accelerator."

The car roared.

"Not so fast," he said, laughing. His breath was warm against my leg. I didn't dare move.

His hand covered mine on the gearshift and moved it out of Park. I was so cautious in applying the accelerator that we inched forward on the gravel with a popping sound, as if we were driving over bubble wrap.

"*Yellah*," he said. "Let's go. We're alone."

I shrieked in delight as the car burst into the next gear and accelerated suddenly. I drove down the empty road into the unlit desert until all we could see was disappearing road ahead of the front lights. That was probably the most exhilarating moment of all, being so completely alone in the dark, no sound except our breath and the hum of the engine, nobody watching to tell us about the laws we were breaking.

Eventually, I pulled over to the side and put the car in Park.

"Amazing, isn't it?"

I nodded. I didn't know what to say. I got out of the car and jumped up and down like a six-year-old. I didn't know what to do with myself. Ahmed got out of his side and watched me, his grin shining in the moonlight. Without thinking about it, I threw my arms around his neck and said, "Thank you, thank you, *thank you!*"

Ahmed laughed and hugged me close. Only then did I realize I had never done this, hugged a boy, and this was probably *zina*, but there was something electric between us. I couldn't pull away.

It was over almost instantly, and we jumped apart as if we'd been caught.

"Sorry," we said together. We were both breathing heavily.

"We can't," I said, just as he said, "We shouldn't."

I was trembling. Feeling reckless and bitter, frightened and furious, I said, "Because of Mishail?"

I saw several emotions cross his face, most of which I couldn't understand in the dark. My ears burned.

"Mishail is just another girl to me," he said with a shrug. "She's a giggly, spoiled child who rebels to get attention. Just like Daria. You're not like them."

My heart soared even as my mind filled with doubt.

"But this is real," he said, grabbing my shoulders. "All of us out there? We're on the same side. We're working on a plan. And when it's done, *then*—"

"Then?" I asked, heart in my throat.

"Then," he said, like a promise.

We got back in the car. Ahmed taught me how to turn it around until it was pointed at the group. I drove us back, bringing the car to a neat stop exactly where it used to be.

"You're a natural," Ahmed said, coming over to my side as we got out. My legs were shaking, and his warm hand clasped the back of my neck in affection. It steadied me. Someone made a whooping noise, as if cheering us on. "Do you see it now? Here we can do anything we want. We're real men. But there"—he pointed to the city, a shimmering necklace of golden lights in the distance—"we're just *wiran*. Ladyboys who do what we're told."

In the periphery of my vision, I saw Coca-Cola, the guy who'd "danced" for me, head out into the desert, his arms around another boy. Something about the way they moved made me uneasy.

"What are they doing?" I asked Ahmed.

He didn't answer; he just gave me a patient smile, as if waiting for me to understand something that was obvious.

"*Oh.*"

"We can do *anything* we want," he said again with a meaningful glance.

13

RAMADAN

There is a saying in Najd that a woman who has half a man's heart has twice her sister's share. My future as a lawyer was probably doomed, but I still knew all the permutations and combinations of the law—how it took two women to bear witness but only one man, and that women usually got half their brothers' inheritance, except in special circumstances where we got double, and those I had bookmarked by folding pages in our textbook.

When the law stated that a man could marry four women and have a few concubines besides through *misyar* marriages, a boy was not just well within his rights to love two girls, he was practically a saint for choosing only two.

Still, by the time Ramadan slid into place in November with that first aching prayer, I hated myself for hungering after the boy my best friend loved, and I hated Ahmed for pouring oil on a flame we could not satisfy.

To see the waxing crescent moon, no thicker than a human hair, was supposed to signal the month of purity, and to know that you had begun it by betraying your best friend for a crime you were committing yourself was to realize that, in the end, Ramadan was about punishment. That maybe, if you spent a month starving and suffering, God could forgive you.

And there was that fact. That I was committing the same crime. There was no way to make myself believe that it was different because I had no father to catch me and no future to lose. Ahmed and I hadn't gone further than a few casual touches, but I had fallen in a different, deeper kind of love.

These days the scent of petrol instantly sent a surge of adrenaline through me. I'd been out with Ahmed only a few times, but each time it had been three hours of being on high alert, looking out for the police and listening to my heart pound in my chest as our car drifted down the empty lanes. Once, we'd gone all the way to the refinery, where hundred-foot flames blazed into the pitch-black sky. When I got home that night, I didn't so much fall asleep as collapse into blissful and boneless nonexistence.

I knew now what Mishail meant when she'd said, *I'm*

finally alive after being buried underground for sixteen years. Fear made us feel alive, and we were intoxicated with rebellion and hunger and our determination not to engage in any *zina*, at least during the holy month. Ahmed and I spent every minute of our time together straining against our attraction, which made it only stronger. Sometimes I could feel him shift an inch toward me in the passenger's seat, and the car would swerve in response. If he was driving, and I'd made him smile, I'd wish he could keep looking at me like that even if it meant we'd die in a crash.

I wasn't going to be missed at home. My mother was busy catering to daily *ifthar* events because of Ramadan, and she assumed I was staying with Mishail. It wasn't as if she'd been paying enough attention to know that anything had changed.

That *everything* had changed.

I knew now that I couldn't trust anyone else to take care of me. And after the things Ahmed said about liking my independent spirit, I didn't want them to. So I walked to Hossein's house and said I wanted to work for him. To learn more of the law, maybe earn enough to put myself through university one day.

If I lived that long.

I understood it now, why the boys in Ahmed's *shabab* careered down the streets yodeling at the top of their lungs. Why they committed their acts of vandalism, spraying scandalous gossip about clerics as graffiti along the manicured storefronts of Malaz. Most shops didn't open until sunset, when the day's fast was broken, so from dawn to dusk the metal shutters let us know that the powerful Imam Ibn Abbas had secretly married his sister, or that the youngest Rashid was addicted to cocaine coming in from Yemen, all with a short link to some site that had a video or a photo as proof but would be online for only a day.

During Ramadan, the city came alive at night, and we were out in the desert until two or three in the morning. The wilder boys, like Coca-Cola, would shout out ideas to defame or assassinate powerful authorities, while the more peaceful ones would recite their favorite poems, reminding us that these were the words others had been jailed for. Died for.

Ahmed sang the first verse from Kashgari's letter to the prophet Muhammad: "On your birthday, I will say that I have loved the rebel in you, that you've always been a source of inspiration to me, and that I do not like the halos of divinity around you. I shall not pray for you."

There were cheers, and I heard my father's name among them. I shivered. These verses were filled with so much love for our prophet, and yet the poet had been called an apostate and excommunicated from the Muslim community, the *ummah*, for his disrespect. It made no sense.

The next verse was spoken by the boy who had gone into the darkness with Coca-Cola that first night. "On your birthday, I find you wherever I turn. I will say that I have loved aspects of you, hated others, and could not understand many more."

I sang the last verse, eager to show that I was one of them. I knew the words of the rebels, and I was ready to live by them. "On your birthday, I shall not bow to you. I shall not kiss your hand. Rather, I shall shake it as equals do and smile at you as you smile at me. I shall speak to you as a friend, no more."

"If you were going to die tomorrow, what would you regret not doing today?" Ahmed asked me as we drove away from the group. I knew the answer he wanted from me, but I wasn't ready to give it.

"It's not this world but the next one I'm worried about," I muttered, feeling a prick of guilt. Driving around and singing forbidden poetry was one thing, breaking only those man-made laws that we thought were stupid. But slandering clerics was a sin, and touching a non-*mahram* boy was *zina* that would take you straight to hell. And that was just what we'd already done. As for all the things I wanted to do, Mishail's words were proving prophetic. It was as if having such heavy gates and veils on our bodies had allowed our minds to wander with complete freedom. The things I dreamed of doing with Ahmed would not just cost me my life but would damn my soul forever in the eyes of God.

I kept seeing him anyway.

As I put on the white *thobe* that belonged to my father, I noted that I was his height now. I wondered if Ahmed liked me only because I looked so much like him. I knew I was a hypocrite, allowing myself the very same madness I'd denied Mishail. And it was madness, a consuming obsession that drove me to Ahmed night after night. Not an obsession with *him*, I told myself. It was something more subtle than that. The scars on my forearms were nearly invisible now, but I could still remember what it had felt like, the unbelievable rush of fear, blood, and pain and the bliss that followed it, before the headmistress and her infuriating reasonableness got in the way.

Life had become unbearable, so I'd learned not to fear death. It was as if I'd jumped off a roof, and *Qayamat*, the Day of Judgment, when we'd stand before God and answer for what we'd done, was the ground I was hurtling toward. But there was no more use in fighting it than there was in screaming after I'd jumped. I might as well make peace with my end.

"Maybe we should give up," I said to Ahmed one night when I was feeling more conflicted than usual. Someone had suggested holding protests at Justice Square, the way the Egyptians had at Tahrir. But that square patch of sand outside the courthouse was also called Chop-Chop Square because it was where prisoners were executed. More than five people gathering in public was forbidden by law. Even standing where so many had died felt like a crime.

I said, "You could go to university. You could leave the country."

I meant, *You're not a girl, you're not stuck like me.* I meant, *Why are you staying with me when you don't have to?*

He laughed as if I'd said something very childish.

"Do you really think you could ever leave this?" he asked as we slipped between two cliffs to burst upon a star-studded sky. I gasped. Above our heads the star known as *Yad al-Jauza*, the hand of Orion, glowed a fiery orange. It was humbling to look at the cloudless desert sky, to feel so tiny in the universe. *This*, this was God. Not the bearded face of a *muttawa*. Not the rules that suffocated us, not the stupid and pointless shops of Faisaliyah with the designer handbags I couldn't afford and didn't need. Religion was what I felt now, what I could *only* ever feel out in the desert.

Why couldn't we just do what we wanted and believe what we wanted and be left alone? There was enough space in the desert for us all. It stretched out around us, asking nothing, all these sunset-red cliffs and sudden, proud trees and *wadis* where shepherds led their flock to newly discovered springs.

"Yes, I *could* go to university," Ahmed said. "I could study hard to become a doctor only to have my seat go to someone with *wasta*. I could go to America and become a taxi driver. I could give up on the world altogether and join *them*."

He didn't have to explain who *they* were. The rest of the bin Ladens might care more about buying towers of condominiums than blowing them up, but the legacy of *that* one still endured. Sometimes I wondered how my government could be so blind. It had made alcohol illegal, and so people got drunk every night on *sid* they made at home in bathtubs and carried around in Rausch sparkling apple-juice bottles. *Zina*, or fornication, was illegal, and so the average person got divorced at least two times, at least according to Hossein's client list. And as for joining *them*, I might not be allowed to go to university without my guardian's consent, but I could buy a gun in Batha with just six months of lunch money, no questions asked.

I thought of how on every birthday my father would present me with books he had smuggled in or downloaded and printed at the office for my sake, books that were banned for sedition. He always gave them to me along with those famous words of the prophet that meant all those things that fathers in this country were not allowed to say to their daughters.

If a daughter is born to a person and he brings her up, gives her a good education and trains her in the arts of life, I shall myself stand between him and hellfire.

"Or you could teach. Start a school," I said. "Teach children something different, maybe they'll grow up to be different."

Ahmed smiled at me, that affectionate sidelong glance I now lived for.

"Most people aren't worth the trouble," he said. "But you're definitely your father's daughter."

I fell silent, aching with loss. I remembered what my

father had said to Maryam Madam on parent-teacher night, his soul shining out of his slanted eyes as he said rebellion was in our nature. "Me against my brother. Me and my brother against the tribe. Me and my tribe against the world. That is how the proverb goes, is it not?"

"There is another way," Maryam Madam had answered. "Tie a man in chains and he will show you the extent of his strength. Give a woman her freedom and she will show you the extent of her wisdom."

My father had thrown back his head and laughed, as if he had finally found his match.

"He always dreamed of starting a school," I admitted, and my eyes filled with tears I hadn't shed for him in years. *"Aiyi shakhrasa aiyi darrasa,* he would say. Anybody, any study."

"So if you were going to die tomorrow," Ahmed asked again as he drove me home.

Nothing would stop me today, I thought, and my heart felt as if it had been burned pure.

14

MULTAZIMAT

There is only one difference between girls and boys," Mishail said, loudly enough that I could hear her even though she was on the other side of the room. "Every boy wants to walk where no other man has ever walked, to have what no other boy has ever had. Every girl wants to be where all the other girls are, to have what they have."

There was a hum of agreement among her set. I felt another pang of guilt, followed immediately by anger. Why should I be the one to give in?

Mishail's triumphant return to school after her two-week suspension was like something out of a novel. She wore her crime like a crown, refusing to tell anyone what she had done to merit the punishment. The rumors that grew around her had the complexity of the desert rose, sand twisting upon itself until it formed intriguing crystals in the shape of flowers. The first rumor I heard was that she had climbed out her window to meet her lover at a mixed-gender restaurant and had been caught by *muttaween*. Another was that upon her suspension, she had been sent to Paris to her aunt and that the two of them had tasted champagne and gone out with French boys. Mishail fueled this latter rumor by saying calmly, "After you've tasted real champagne, you can't even look at a Pepsi without feeling like vomiting."

She had given up soft drinks and chocolates entirely, and her skin glowed as if it had been polished with honey. She walked proudly and confidently, as if she had nothing to be ashamed of. But the thing that broke my heart was the way she smiled at me. It was an absent, pitying smile, the kind a queen would give to the beggars who chewed on their *miswak* sticks as they sat on the pavement. Mishail wasn't just at peace without me, she was *happy*.

The only person unhappier than me was Daria. She was snapping at everyone these days, particularly at Aisha for making mistakes in law class. Most people probably thought it was the stress of the debate. I felt it was because Daria had seen Mishail as her sidekick and didn't want anyone but herself at the center. I almost felt sorry for her.

After sixteen years, I had learned that Mishail would always be the sun around which we all revolved. Even now, when I hated her for her happiness, when I wished for something to happen that would make her miss me as much as I missed her, when Ahmed dropped me off at home with a simple good night instead of saying something romantic and I wondered whether he was still texting Mishail, I knew that she was and would always be the center of our world, a goddess among ordinary girls.

Mishail sat on a table in the corner of the room. It was recess and raining outside, so we were all indoors, unsupervised. Zainab, Sofia, and nearly a dozen other girls sat in chairs around Mishail.

"Mishy, I have a philosophical question," Zainab said hesitantly, and I snapped my pencil in half at the casual confidence with which that pear-shaped princess used *my* nickname for *my* best friend.

I glared at Mishail, but she either pretended not to notice or had finally perfected her mask so even I couldn't see within.

Zainab continued, "Mahmoud says that he wants women to be educated and modern, and he's not one of those guys who expects his wife to wear a *hijab* in public. But his sister told me that it was just what he said because he wanted the woman to *choose* to stay at home and guard herself from other men out of love and submission to him. She said that there had been another woman, who did what Mahmoud *said* he wanted. She acted modern, and then he broke off the engagement because he thought she was cheap. What do you think I should do?"

"A man's soul is divided," Mishail said, as if issuing a *fatwa*. "A man is always questioning whether to follow his head or his heart. The Arab man believes in his head that he wants a modern wife who is educated, but do you see those kinds of girls"—she coughed a word that sounded like my name, and some of the girls laughed—"getting proposals or even a love letter? That's because deep in his heart, a man wants to feel powerful, and in this country, the only way he can be powerful is if someone else is under him. So your sister-in-law is right. You're in the *milkah* period now, so Mahmoud's talking from his head. After the marriage is final, he'll speak from his heart."

My hands clenched in fists. I couldn't bear much more of this. I didn't dare look up to see if anyone was on my side. I knew what the answer was likely to be. Worst of all, Mishail's words had the sting of truth. Ahmed laughed at my jokes, said he loved talking to me, said that he had never felt such a close connection with anyone. But he never called me beautiful. I was starting to wonder if he didn't feel the same electricity. If I was starting to be as familiar as a sister.

As if reading my thoughts, Mishail said, "The key to a man's heart is to be helpless. Let him save you and protect you. Men need to be needed. Otherwise, they'll think you're one of the *boyat*, nothing but a tomboy sidekick. What do you want as a gift, a necklace or a necktie?"

I stormed out of the classroom at the laughter that followed. How could she? As if I had a choice about my situation, as if I *wanted* to be treated like a boy.

As soon as I entered the bathroom, I realized I had walked in on another clique I wasn't part of. Bilquis hurriedly shushed the four girls around her into silence. I rolled my eyes. It had been an impressive feat, really, how Bilquis had also converted her humiliation into a badge of honor. Bilquis hadn't soiled her pants because she was *shy*, it was because she was *religious*. Bilquis and her mother weren't fossils stuck in an old, traditional age. They were *multazimat*, "committed to Islam," a term Bilquis used nearly every day now to justify all sorts of things, but mostly to walk around with a saintly look of peace that apparently came from knowing that everyone else was going to hell.

Now she had her own little group of religious nuts who followed her around. They made disapproving clucking noises whenever they heard any mention of boys, love, or marriage, sometimes making the younger girls cry at lunch by telling them they would go to hell for wearing friendship bracelets.

Bilquis walked up to me with her arms crossed against her chest. "I haven't forgotten how you tried to get me to commit *haraam*," she said, using the traditional Arabic of the preachers. "It is said, *Let them not stamp their feet so as to reveal their adornment*. I haven't forgotten how you pranced about in the open."

"You know what they say, an elephant never forgets," I said.

Bilquis moved forward as if to slap me, but I ducked.

"Still haven't learned how to run?" I said, and darted out of the bathroom. My blood was pounding again. It had felt good to insult Bilquis. For those few moments I hadn't been hurting over Mishail. But soon that pleasure subsided, and I felt worse than I had before. How strange it was that guilt and anger went together so well, like salt and lime! I hated everything and everyone these days, and that hate burned so bright it was molding me into someone new. Someone who was sharp but proud of it, who wore a knife around her heart as if it were a gold brooch.

I returned to class just in time to hear Daria say to Mishail's group, "Don't be silly. Naseema Madam is blind as a bat. She hides behind her dirty *hijab* so she won't have to see the truth."

"And what's that?" asked Munira.

Daria seemed to sense that I could hear her, because she looked at me and said, "I'm not about to tell you in front of that traitor."

Mishail laughed, and I turned away to hide my burning face.

"Please?" Munira begged. "You can't just leave it like

that. Do you really know a secret, or are you just making it up to get attention?"

Daria fumed and said, "Have you never wondered how a woman as poor and stupid and traditional as Naseema became headmistress of a top school? Why so many princes and government ministers donated money to keep the school running and admit more girls, when the woman has neither brains nor *wasta*? Why Najd National was targeted for total destruction and this school had only a few broken windows? If you can't put it all together, you're as stupid as she is."

There was silence. Everyone shifted uneasily. Even Mishail was frowning. But I could tell none of the other girls had made the connection Daria wanted them to. The fact that I understood only made me feel worse. No decent mind would have gone there, and no woman should have been able to understand as quickly as I had. But one day, when I'd been more miserable than usual about my lack of a future, Ahmed, to cheer me up, told me about the parties in Bahrain where women who had been promised internships with the government were instead sold into service on cruise ships to please foreign diplomats and spy on them. Those girls needed to speak fluent Arabic and English, and they needed to be as beautiful as they were poor.

Daria's eyes met mine. She saw that I now knew, and her eyes grew wide and afraid. She said quickly, "Never mind. Leave me alone," and turned to her book.

"I don't understand," Aisha said.

"That's because you're an idiot," Daria said through her teeth.

"I'm sorry," Aisha said, her voice shaking. "I don't know why everything I say makes you angry. I was just trying to—"

"Would you *shut up*, you incredible waste of space? It's bad enough we're going to lose because you can't remember more than six *hadith* at a time, do you have to keep annoying me with your screeching voice?"

Batool Madam walked in at just that moment. She reeled as if struck, and then seemed to collect herself. She marched over to Daria and grabbed her by the ear and dragged her out of class, telling us to behave while she was out.

The room exploded in whispers and muttering. I saw tears fall from Aisha's eyes onto her law textbook. I went to sit beside her in Daria's empty chair.

"I'm fine," Aisha said. "I know she's just stressed. She doesn't hate me, does she?"

I didn't answer; I just rubbed her back. My head was spinning with the sickening realization of why Daria acted the way she did, why she was so boy crazy. Where she had first got her experience.

"Everyone hates me," Aisha sobbed. "Mishail hates me because I took her place. You hate me because you know you're better than me at law."

"I don't hate you," I said. I felt the sharp edges of my heart soften just a little. It wasn't fair that Aisha had been chosen over me. But it also wasn't fair that Aisha was bearing the punishment for something that wasn't her fault. We were all fighting one another for a window out of hell. *Me against my sisters.*

It had to stop.

15

KHULA

That weekend, I could tell by the charge in the air that my mother was lying to me again. I was told to pack blankets and pillows into cardboard boxes that had been marked *Fragile*. Really? My mother said the boxes had always been marked that way, but I could still smell the marker in the air.

She was now in the kitchen making a picnic lunch, and Fatima Aunty was chewing on a carrot (her latest diet involved doing this all day, and she was turning orange as a result) and offering her opinion on our decision to spend the day in the desert with the Hossein family.

"Far be it from me to tell you how to live your life," Fatima Aunty began, as she always did when she wanted to pull rank. She was my father's older sister, and that put her above his wife in status. "It's just, what will people say? Going out with a non-*mahram* man on a Friday? Even if his wife is there, what can she do if . . ."

Fatima Aunty trailed off when she saw me in the doorway.

"It's just for a few hours, in open daylight," my mother said, her eyes on me, warning me not to mention the blankets and pillows. As if I were that stupid.

Fatima Aunty sighed, and my mother's shoulders pinched upward. The tension in the room was so high that when the doorbell rang, I flinched. I let Faraz in to help carry the boxes down to the car.

"And that's another thing," Fatima Aunty said in a whisper so loud it was clearly meant for Faraz's ears. "Why are they borrowing your glassware to throw a party?"

"Do you see us throwing a party?" my mother asked. "Why can't they use what we're not using?"

When we were climbing down the stairs with the boxes, Faraz asked, "What's her problem?"

"Nobody to claw at," I said. My hands were itching. I placed the boxes in the flatbed of the pickup and took the stairs two at a time to avoid missing the explosion I knew was about to occur.

"They act like brother and sister, as if they were *mahram*," Fatima Aunty was saying. "It's completely inappropriate for Leena to be without her *abaya* around him."

"You said it yourself, they act like they're brother and sister. Isn't that the whole point of *mahram*, that it is meant for family?"

"I just want to make sure you're not vulnerable. In your situation—"

"You're not in my situation. Now please call your driver to have him pull up. I don't want to keep them waiting."

Fatima Aunty squawked in protest. She said, "I was going to stay here and wait for you to get back."

I stood at the entrance of the room, eyes fixed on my mother. I knew Fatima Aunty could tell something was up. She had come to check in on us. Her offer to stay and wait was nothing more than policing. She might not have seen the blankets in the back of the truck, but she must have had a vague intuition that we weren't coming home that night.

My mother smiled, the bone-chilling and ruthless smile that I had come to recognize as meaning that the next words would land with the crisp deadliness of lightning.

"I'm sorry that your infertility has made you feel the need to mother me. But I don't need you."

Fatima Aunty gasped. A shiver passed through me. I understood now why my mother always had such frustration in her voice when she said I was sharp. I had learned my anger from her.

I fixed my eyes on Fatima Aunty's red face, on the fat and quivering lower lip that I loathed for its weakness.

Fight back, I pleaded inwardly. *Fight back. She wants you to.*

"I just—how can you say such a thing? I'm here because I *love* you."

My mother put on her *abaya* and handed a pile of black silk over to Fatima Aunty with an expectant eyebrow.

"If you're going to be like this, I'll—see if I care! I'll never come back! I'll tell Hadi, and I'll never visit, I'll never—"

My mother grinned.

Fatima Aunty marched out, texting her driver furiously. She brushed past me on the way out, her face so orange that it appeared her headscarf was choking her.

"Let's go," my mother said. She had a determined look in her eyes, the kind that I knew spelled death for anything or anyone that got in her way. It was the same look she had when she put bleaching powder on the kitchen floor and sprayed Windex on the cockroaches to melt them into dust while they were still alive.

I followed quietly, taking my place by the window in the back, separated from Faraz by my mother, who sat in the middle. Nobody spoke, although my mother was having some sort of conversation with the Hosseins, in the front seat, that consisted purely of exchanged looks. Rather than hazard a guess, I looked out the open window, glad of any chance to be outside. In Riyadh, with its geometrically designed, wide roads, pedestrians were rarely if at all present. Ahmed said it was because of the law against public gatherings, enforced by the *mahabith*.

We passed through the poorer districts on the outskirts of the city, where the foreign laborers stayed in cramped hovels. Men with rubbery red skin lounged around *bakhalas*, spitting out tobacco juice or cleaning their teeth with twigs as they waited for work. Young immigrant boys with white mesh caps rode bicycles through narrow streets, driving me mad with jealousy. Women were allowed to ride bicycles only if escorted by a *mahram*. Not that much bicycling was likely to happen with an *abaya* in the way.

Finally, we were out of the city, heading toward the red mountains. The landscape was barren and empty to the horizon in every direction, and yet it filled me with a sense of possibility. Beyond the city limits, past the police, were the farmlands and pastures of the bedouin who lived off the land. Sometimes I found myself envious of them, even though they were poor, especially the young girls who stayed behind to milk the goats and tend to the camels.

Ahead, the sun shone so brightly that it created a mirage, as if a thin film of water was on the smooth road. Small shacks dotted the roadside, where men lounged in the shade alongside gallons of water and crates of soda cans. And then those, too, disappeared, and we were well into the Najd plateau. Swirls of dust whipped up in little tornadoes, enchanting inverted pyramids that soared arrogantly into the sky.

Hossein took an exit, leaving behind the paved road for a flat path carved by the tires of other trucks. My mother took off her headscarf, shaking her hair loose with a look of mute obstinacy. We stopped in a clearing that was hidden from the road by a large hill. The adults pulled out a mat and blankets and set up a picnic in the shade of the truck. I wandered around, exploring the clearing, glad to stretch my legs and just be outside. Faraz sat in the flatbed of the truck, reading some university-preparation book. I didn't look at it too closely, because it would only make me jealous. He was due to hear back soon about whether he'd been accepted.

I heard my mother call me. There was something strangled about her voice, as if she was trying very hard not to show her emotions. I hurried back.

To my surprise, all she said was, "Faraz, why don't you try teaching Leena how to drive."

For a moment Faraz and I looked at each other as if confirming we hadn't imagined that.

"You just want us to go away so you can talk in peace," I said.

"So?" my mother said with the same strained voice, and turned away as if the decision had been made.

I got in the truck. I knew better than to argue with her when she was in that mood. We'd both end up saying the most horrible things to each other. I was so preoccupied with trying to understand what was going on that I forgot

I wasn't supposed to know how to drive. I had adjusted the seat and mirrors for my height and turned the key in the ignition before I realized Faraz was supposed to teach me how to do those things.

It was too late. My secret was out. Faraz's face showed that not only had he figured out that I knew what I was doing, but he also had a pretty good idea I'd been doing this a lot, and recently.

My heart skipped a beat. I was about to beg him not to say anything when he said quietly so only I'd hear, "If you step hard on the accelerator, the truck will jump. It's a common mistake people make when they're first learning. It usually makes them scream a little."

I obeyed, overcome with gratitude. We moved forward in a jerk, and I squealed loud enough for the adults to hear. They laughed and told us to have fun. My ears burned.

We drove out of earshot before I said, "You aren't going to ask?"

"Not unless you want me to," he said. I shook my head. He continued, "Don't drive at such a steady speed, then."

I laughed and relaxed, slowing and speeding up inconsistently as if I were new at this.

"Do you know what they're talking about?" I asked.

"Yes," Faraz said. "It's what they always talk about. Your future."

"Oh," I said, and my voice shook. I wanted to ask what he knew, what they said, but I couldn't bring myself to ask.

"I'll tell you if you really want to know," he said, looking ahead instead of at me. "But not while you're driving. And there are things you might not want to know."

His voice had a twinge of hurt, and I wondered what that was about. He was right, though. There were certain things it was better not to know. What I'd learned about Daria, about the secrets of Najd National, had made me sick with anger and disgust that had no outlet. I couldn't even talk to Ahmed about it. The idea of talking to a *boy* about that stuff was completely impossible.

"When?" I asked Faraz. "When can you tell me?"

"Tonight, after they're asleep. If you can stay awake, meet me behind that." He pointed to a mushroom-shaped rock.

The evening passed so slowly that I thought I would die of anxiety. I watched my mother carefully as she helped Faraz's mother with the cooking, but they let nothing slip. They cooked the meat the bedouin way, burying it in foil amid the sun-baked stones of an extinguished fire pit to let it roast over the course of hours. My mother avoided looking at me, so I knew she was upset about something.

We set up three tents, one for Faraz's parents, one for me and my mother, and one for Faraz. It took every bit of my concentration to escape the tent without waking her up, and I padded all the way over quietly to the rock that was lit up in the moonlight before I realized my teeth were chattering. Faraz was already there, and when he saw that

I'd come wearing the clothes I'd gone to sleep in, he took the blanket he had wrapped around himself and put it around my shoulders.

I stammered a surprised thanks.

"Are you really sure you want to know?" he whispered.

I nodded, and then realized he probably couldn't see it, so I said, "Yes."

"Your mother wants a divorce," he said.

I made a startled sound, and Faraz leaped up and clapped his hand over my mouth. I felt faint with cold and shock. It couldn't be. My knees shook, and Faraz's other arm came around my waist to hold me up.

"You promise you won't be so loud if I let go?"

I nodded, sinking to the ground. I felt that same floating sensation I'd had in the headmistress's office, the words coming from a distance. I was numb.

"The trouble is that she can't actually sue for *khula* without your father's consent. All the other requirements can be met."

My mind scrambled to remember the requirements for *khula*. In other countries, women had the right to divorce without the husband's consent. It was known as *talaaq-i-tafweez*. But not here. In addition, here the wife had to pay her husband back her *mahr*, the bride-price she had been gifted with upon marriage. No wonder she'd been working so hard. All those *ifthar* parties at Ramadan, when I thought she was just keeping herself busy, she'd been collecting the required amount. She'd never said a word.

Faraz said, "In Yemen, the woman is granted a divorce if the husband is in prison for some number of years, but we don't have that law here. If the husband doesn't consent—"

"It's up to the judge," I finished. "How can she do this?"

"It's a gamble," Faraz said. "I think she believes your father won't consent. That he'll realize where he belongs, sign the *taahud*, and come home. Because, if she gets the *khula*, she also gets custody of you."

I felt a jolt of pride underneath my anger. It was a smart plan.

"But if he accepts—" I couldn't finish that sentence. I couldn't believe that my father would let that happen.

"You know better than me how that ends," Faraz said. He wouldn't look at me. I understood his embarrassment. My mother's catering business would lose clients. My mother wouldn't be able to stay in the house or keep her bank account. I would never find a husband or a job when people found out that my parents were divorced. We would have to start over in Hofuf with the women refugees (*and eat cockroaches*), and that was if we even got to Hofuf. We wouldn't be able to travel without permission. In all likelihood, we'd end up on the streets.

"We have to stop her," I said, shaking my head helplessly. It was too insane a risk.

"I think there's another plan," Faraz said hesitantly. "It was an idea my father had, right when they asked you and me to go away. I don't know the details for sure, but I can guess."

"What is it?" I asked. Faraz didn't answer. I grabbed his collar. "Tell me!"

"*Shhh!*" he said. His hands came up around mine and gently pulled them off. The warmth of his hands made me realize again how cold I was. But I couldn't bear his pitying kindness. I snatched my hands away.

"There's only one other person who can make him come home."

I waited, but still Faraz hesitated. I wondered why he wouldn't tell me. What could be worse than divorce? My mind wasn't working, and my thoughts spun around in hazy circles, trying to put the pieces together.

"That's what my father said," Faraz continued. "That there was just one other person. Then your mother said she would never let another woman pay for her happiness."

"What does that mean?" I asked, pulling the blanket close around me.

"I don't know."

"You said you had a guess." I knew I was begging, my voice hoarse with despair.

Faraz sighed. "It's only a guess. The only other woman who has any influence over your father is you. I think . . . I think they mean to get you married, to someone powerful, ideally in government. Your father would never consent to something like that. He'd die first."

I shuddered. It was too absurd.

"That won't work. I'd have to consent, too," I said.

"Besides, who in government would want to marry the daughter of a jailed rebel?"

"Leena, there's something else you should know," Faraz said, shifting awkwardly in the sand as if he needed to pee.

"Yes?"

"I got accepted to Qaraouine."

My heart skipped a beat. I was glad that it was dark and that he couldn't see that my immediate reaction was a wild and jealous fury. It broke my heart that Qaraouine, the university started by a woman, was now closed to us all. And *Faraz* had gotten in, while I wasn't allowed to apply!

"I don't know how I got in," Faraz said, sounding amazed. "Everyone else has already done something amazing with their lives. Helped refugees in Jordan and Egypt, petitioned the United Nations, gone on national television to debate world politics. I've barely made it through high school, and you know exactly how good I am at law. You started off behind me, and now I swear you're better at it than my father."

"Congratulations," I said, choking with the effort not to cry.

"I don't know what your plans are for the future, but if you wanted to come with me—"

"How?" I snarled, feeling far too breakable to be kind about it. "I can't even apply. Even if I got in, I couldn't pay. If I got a scholarship, I wouldn't be allowed to accept it.

And I can't leave the country without a guardian, and even if my father did get out of jail, it would be by signing the *taahud*, which we know means he wouldn't be allowed to leave the country. So how exactly am I supposed to come with you? And what am I supposed to do while I'm there, count chickens?"

For a long time Faraz said nothing. He seemed to stop and start sentences in his head, as if he had an idea in his mind but didn't want to say it. In the end, all he said was, "If you wanted to come, if you found a way, I would like for you to come with me. That's all. No pressure."

Then he got up and walked off, his shoulders hunched in defeat.

16

SHILLAH

The *shillah* was my idea, but the contract was Aisha's, naturally. It was simple, but we started it with *Bismillah-ur-Rahman-ur-Rahim*, which meant *In the name of God, the beneficent, the merciful*, so breaking it was unthinkable.

We wrote out the contract while sitting on the ledge outside the bathroom window, where the pellet gun and bag of bullets gathered dust. It was my first day back after the weekend camping in the desert with the Hossein family, and I really needed to talk to *someone*. I didn't know how boys did it, kept secrets that were so explosive they could shatter us in an instant. I felt the pressure building inside me, and I didn't know how long it would be before I burst from holding it all in.

As for Aisha, she was always the practical one. I took her to the ledge after Daria blew up at her yet again for confusing *jihad* and *itjihad*, which was a very reasonable mistake that everyone made at least once, the way anyone learning English started off thinking *inflammable* meant the opposite of *flammable*. But Daria had called Aisha the weight around her feet that would drown us all. Aisha burst into tears, and I just couldn't take it anymore.

I said we should form a secret society, but only invite outcasts. Collect the people who weren't so religious that they'd be absorbed into the Bilquis Bubble, but who, for whatever reason, weren't part of the liberal Daria-Mishail-Zainab set, either.

Aisha said the hard part would not be getting people to join, but getting them to stay, and stay true when things got hard. We needed a contract that would guarantee our safety. Otherwise, what was to stop someone from betraying the others' secrets if they decided someday to leave the *shillah*? Hadn't Daria betrayed Bilquis exactly this way?

So the contract we drew up required that girls who joined had to share a secret that they had told no one else and had to give evidence of it to the others for safekeeping. I shared a print of the photo I'd had Ahmed take of me with his cell phone (unlike us, *boys* did not have a busted camera on *their* phones). In it I was unveiled and behind the wheel, wearing large reflective sunglasses, my hair flying loose behind me as if I were a movie star.

Aisha gave me love letters she had received from a cousin in Dubai she hoped to marry one day.

The second rule written into the contract was that we would do whatever we could to help the others in the *shillah* and never knowingly harm them. Rule three contained proceedings for new members. Besides submitting acceptable evidence of their trespasses, at least three existing members would have to agree that the new person could be included. (Which I pointed out was ridiculous since there were only two of us, but Aisha seemed convinced that was a temporary situation.)

The remaining rules were silly, but for Aisha's sake I signed to agree that once we joined, only death could end our membership, and that if a new member was invited and refused, she could not ask again for one year. I didn't want to point out that since we were seniors, after we left school in the spring, some of us would end up housewives never to be seen again while others would do their best to leave the country and never come back, so planning a multi-year contract was a little too optimistic.

I didn't tell Aisha about my mother's plan to get divorced, though. Only naive *garawiyya* told all their secrets to new friends, starting with the most shameful. But starting a *shillah*, or any friendship, as I'd learned from Mishail, was like a dance. You had to find out how you fit with the other person, then you had to find the beat, and then came the first phase of the new friendship, where you were surprised at how well you moved together, how much you agreed on. It was only after you found that groove that you could test its strength.

The secrets we started with were the ones we were actually proud of. Driving, love, romance, and adventure. Just as Mishail had shown me her lace underwear stuffed in the air conditioner, where they lay in wait for the right day, I showed Aisha a photo of Ahmed that he had posted on a site that allowed us to share pictures but see them only once. Then the photos were automatically deleted, exploding in a puff of virtual smoke, saving us all from future ruin. Aisha used it to share a photo of her cousin Nasser and cursed his pale, hairless skin.

"He's a Hejazi man; I don't know if he'll ever change," she said, as if she didn't delight in exactly that paleness.

"Did you really want someone who looks as if he's loafing around under the sun like a jobless person?" I retorted, even though I loved Ahmed's dark skin and the way his eyes shone.

Then came the honeymoon phase. In Riyadh, girls courted one another the way we wished boys would court us. We gave one another heart-shaped necklaces that had our names engraved on them, necklaces that we hid under our *hijab* because they were forbidden at school. We dressed up and wore makeup and went to women-only restaurants in the mall. We complimented one another on our style. Aisha had always wanted to eat at Herfy, but her father, the doctor, strictly forbade it for health reasons, so one evening we went there as an excursion.

It turned out Aisha hated the food, but she laughed so hard it was worth it just for that. At the end, while I drank her milk shake because she couldn't handle any more, she put in the final seal and said, "Leena, can I be serious with you? I need your help with something."

"Anything," I said, because that was the whole point of a secret society.

"I need you to help me with this debate. I know it's asking a lot. I mean, this was always your dream, not mine. My dreams are of medicine, not law."

"What changed?"

"I wanted to be a doctor. Especially a women's doctor. My father's one, you know. He always said it was a sign, and why Allah gave him three daughters."

She didn't say anything for a while, so I said awkwardly, "Becoming a doctor would be a great accomplishment."

"Maybe," she said, frowning as if she were trying to convince herself. "It's not the same thing as power. My older brother was arrested recently. My mother said he'd been posting on a blog, but I don't even know if that's true. I think it was something worse, because we tried to pay the fine and they still wouldn't let him go for five whole days. I heard my father yelling on the phone that money was no problem, but we had no *wasta*. He wants to leave the country, go to Dubai, Oman, somewhere that an education can matter more than birth. Anyway, it's why I've been so mixed up recently. I want to be useful, but I don't even know enough about the law to get through class, never mind to make a difference at the *Majlis*. Most days I'm so scared about the future I can't even concentrate."

I squeezed her hand.

"I know you probably wanted a friend who was more fun," she said, squirming. "But I'm not like—"

"I hate malls," I admitted, not letting her finish that sentence with a name I couldn't bear to hear. "This isn't my kind of fun."

And just like that, we found out how we fit. Every evening, Aisha came over to my house just before the *maghreb*. We prayed, ate a snack, and studied until well after the *isha* prayer. Over dinner, which we cooked together, we discussed what we'd studied and tried to make sense of it.

I had lived through Batool the Fool for so long that I knew what not to do. I refused to be the kind of teacher I hated, forcing down *hadiths* into memory to be regurgitated on demand. I wanted to understand the prophet, to shake his hand as an equal, and to love the rebel in him, this lonely man who had shaped our whole world. So I shared the books with Aisha that my father had smuggled into the country from Lebanon and beyond, including the full works of Ibn Rushd, who explained how the law was derived, the sources and reasoning used in each case, all with the intention of helping jurors decide what the law should be. It was like a magic guide to our textbook, which only gave the answers—if X happens, do Y—without explaining the all-important *why*.

The other book we read, in turns or together, sitting in bed with our knees raised and the book between us, was Al-Ghazali's *Alchemy of Happiness*, which was banned in Saudi Arabia because it had lately come back into fashion, selling more copies in Turkey than the Quran. Al-Ghazali had become paralyzed in the middle of his life. Unable to speak, doctors diagnosed him with a serious emotional disorder because he had lost his faith. He had left the Sunni family to join the Sufi mystics, walking away from the distractions of public life to work on self-discipline and surrender.

In the absence of the real boys we loved, we placed the images of these dead men. Aisha preferred Ibn Rushd, who was practical, almost mathematical in his attention to detail.

"He's the kind of man I can trust. The kind of man I'd marry," she said, as if he hadn't been dead for centuries.

"I want the poet," I said. "I want the one who surrenders to his emotions and lets them carry him away."

I was happy with our little *shillah* of two, but Aisha was right to have expected others to join us. There was something magical about what we had, the spark of souls bonded in that perfect friendship that was at the heart of the idea of the *ummah*. The fanatics had stolen and desecrated that word, *ummah*, calling for an international kingdom of Muslims beyond national laws. But the real *ummah* was something I believed everyone of every faith yearned for, the sense that there was something beyond selfishness and petty tribal feuds. It was a connection of minds that Al-Ghazali had sought hundreds of years ago. And although he was dead, I felt his mind had reached mine.

In a month, we were having weekly *halaqas* as if we were in Qaraouine itself, a group of girls bonded partially by our desire for friendship and freedom and bonded more completely by our mutually assured destruction. Aisha and I still studied together on school days, but on the weekends, nearly a dozen girls met secretly, each telling her parents she was at another's house.

We met at a different place every time, just in case there was a raid. We placed chairs and floor-level Arabian sofas by the walls in a large circle facing the center. Every time, the conversation proceeded like the courtship, beginning with the easy topics—food, fashion, and family—and ending with the serious ones. Books and boys.

"I don't know if it's wrong to be a writer," Sofia said. "I've always wanted to be, but what do I even have to write about? Our lives are so dull. Nothing ever happens. I really want to be a journalist, but wouldn't that be complaining about the will of God, airing everyone's dirty laundry for foreigners to laugh at or pity?"

Sofia had recently extricated herself from Mishail's set

and joined us. I didn't trust her at first, because I couldn't understand why she would want to be with me and Aisha when she could be with the glamorous Daria and Mishail.

"Because sometimes I like to be the one telling the stories, not just listening to theirs," she'd said with a smirk and offered up her evidence. She had written a love story in which our favorite superhero, the Egyptian Qahera, found a man who was worthy of her. The Qahera webcomics were forbidden to us, so writing a love story about the burqa-clad bat-woman was certainly illegal.

"Besides," Sofia added, her smirk fading into grim determination, "my father was killed in the Spring. He was a journalist."

"Is it *haraam* to write stories?" asked Rasha, a whip-smart girl from the junior class who had won a national Quran recitation competition and had found her way into our *shillah* by the ingeniousness of her crime. She had entered the competition purely for the prize money, which she used to buy prepaid phones that could not be traced by the Ministry of the Interior. She had given us these phones so we could contact one another safely.

"Why would you think that, sweetie?" I asked her.

"Because I don't know if it counts as telling a lie. If it doesn't, then maybe Sofia can write about things without giving away any real secrets."

"It only counts as a lie if you pretend it isn't just a story," I said. "And that's a great idea."

Rasha glowed with pleasure. It struck me how easy it was to be generous with affection, and how the more I gave the more I received. We had each been in our corners, hoarding the tiny slice of love we still had, but together we had more than enough for everyone.

Another night we were at Sofia's house, and we didn't talk at all, just danced to celebrate the end of the preliminaries, which everyone knew were harder than the actual final exams. Even I joined in, safe in the knowledge that we were all equally graceless, but we weren't dancing to impress a guy or one another but purely out of our own joy.

"I feel bad for having fun," Aisha confessed that night as her driver took us home. "The debate is coming up, and—"

"Oh, be quiet," I said. "Fun *is* the point. Fun is what *they* keep forbidding. Laughter is all there is. It's what keeps us going, it's what we have left to live for, it's why those girls came today. We might die tomorrow if that's God's will. What's the *point* of anything we do?"

Aisha sniffed. I pulled her into a hug and kissed her until she laughed and pulled away.

Still, she had a point. The gnawing anxiety in my stomach told me that I didn't have much time, either. Ahmed had said that the boys would soon put their plan into place. They were waiting for something, but I hadn't been able to figure out what it was, or maybe they were just bragging idly and didn't even have a plan. Meanwhile, my mother was working two or three events a day to make the amount required to pay back her *mahr* and initiate a divorce. In just months, I would write my final exams and graduate from high school.

Time was running out.

17

GARAWIYYA

The results of the preliminaries were posted in the main hallway. Aisha had beaten me to take first rank. I came in second, and Daria was third. Mishail was barely in the top ten. Even Bilquis had done better.

It was the first time anyone had ever done better than me at school. It stung, and for a moment I thought angrily that if I hadn't helped Aisha, she'd never have won. The impure thought lasted only a moment. The next moment, something wonderful happened that made me realize I would never again care about coming first.

Aisha saw her name at the top of the list, stared in disbelief for nearly a minute while everyone whispered anxiously around us, and then she burst into loud tears and threw her arms around my neck.

It was the happiest moment of my entire school life.

The icing on the cake was Daria's fury. I had never thought anyone could be so upset about losing anything. She called us cheats, lovers, teacher's pets, and other more terrible things, then ran into the classroom and shoved the tables and chairs. She kicked the large metal teacher's desk until it formed a dent the size of a football. And then she grabbed her books and ran out of the classroom.

"Where does she think she's going?" Sofia asked. "First period begins in two minutes."

I watched Aisha receive her congratulations without a trace of jealousy. Fifteen minutes later, we were in the middle of history class when the loudspeakers in our hallway requested that Aisha and I go to the headmistress's office.

"What do you think this is about?" Aisha asked as we made our way there.

I shook my head. We knocked and entered the office that had become so familiar to me that I thought I might actually miss it when I graduated. Maryam Madam and Naseema Madam sat behind a desk covered in preliminary-examination papers and the official registration forms for our finals. Daria sat on the other side, her eyes red.

"Sit down, girls."

Maryam Madam looked puzzled, as if she didn't quite

understand what the issue was yet. It was Naseema Madam who spoke.

"I hear that you and Aisha have been taking special lessons in history and law," she said. "And you did not invite Daria."

My eyebrows flew to the ceiling. Was Daria really playing the kicked kitten here after what she'd done to me and Mishail?

"I don't understand, Naseema," Maryam Madam said. "Many students take private lessons from tutors."

"Not at Najd," Naseema Madam said, sounding sulky. "We did not think it was fair for those who could afford it to have an advantage over those who couldn't."

"Oh," Maryam Madam said. She had a strange look on her face, a kind of amazed fondness, as if a child had said something adorable.

I said, "But, ma'am, it's Daria and Aisha who have been taking the special lessons in preparation for the debate. How is *that* fair?"

Aisha fussed with her hands nervously. I discreetly squeezed her finger to let her know I wasn't actually upset with her. I kept my eyes on Maryam Madam, knowing that I'd be able to tell from her face when a storm was coming. She gave me an exasperated look, but she didn't seem angry.

"When you have to speak in front of an audience, you'll receive the same instruction," Maryam Madam said,

adding with a smile, "Not that you have any trouble finding words, right, Leena?"

"Tell her to say where they're taking lessons!" Daria said
in a voice that shook with sobs. "It's not *fair!*"

"We haven't been taking any lessons, you whiner!" I
said. "It's not our fault you're so stupid."

"Leena!" Maryam Madam said. I fell silent immediately, sorry for having lost my temper. But I *hated* Daria so
much I was giddy with it.

"Liar," Daria muttered.

"How dare *you* call *me* a liar after the things you've
done!" I shouted, aware that I was probably making things
worse for myself with the headmistresses, but how many
times was I supposed to let Daria ruin my life and then
insult me? "You call Naseema Madam a blind bat behind
her back while you break every single rule in existence, but
now you're acting like you're the *victim?*"

"Leena, *khalaas!*" Maryam Madam said. *Now* she was
angry. I fell back in my chair, breathing heavily. Naseema
Madam was paler than I'd ever seen her, as if she'd been
slapped.

"How *dare* you speak that way in front of us?" Maryam
Madam said. She was standing now, her fingers clenched
around the edge of her desk.

"Daria would never say anything bad about other
people," Naseema Madam said in a low voice. I felt a pinch
of hatred for her, too, for being so blind. "Don't you know,

at Najd, she was the favorite of every teacher and all the students."

"No wonder," I muttered under my breath. Daria heard me and flinched. I felt the urge to strike at her even harder until she learned not to stand in my way again.

"What's that you said?" Maryam Madam said. "What's wrong with you, Leena? You think I don't see that something's changed? You're being stupid to the point of recklessness, and I don't understand why *now* when you're so close to graduation. Don't you care about your future? About what happens to you? What would your father think?"

I knew this was just Maryam Madam entering Phase Two, but I didn't have the patience to wait until she made it through all her questions and arrived at her total disappointment. Not this time.

"My future?" I said with a bitter laugh. "I don't *have* a future, do I? You and Daria saw to that. I'm not allowed to be part of the debate because *Majlis* members might question the character of a girl whose father is in prison. But Daria? It doesn't matter that she's given her phone number to every guard outside this school, that she gave herself to all the male teachers of Najd National to keep her top grades, none of that matters a bit because . . . why? Are you both really as blind as she says you are? Or does she have some *wasta* that cleanses her of all her sins, in which case, how do I get some of that?"

The old, round clock above the headmistresses' heads ticked loudly in the silence that followed. The second hand moved heavily upward past the large seven, slipping a millimeter downward with every upstroke, as if sagging against gravity.

Maryam Madam was no longer staring at me but *through* me.

Naseema Madam said, "Leena, do you have any evidence that proves what you just said?"

I looked at Aisha out of the corner of my eyes. She shook her head very slightly in warning, so I said nothing. I wasn't going to get Zainab, Mishail, Munira, or any of the others to confess what they knew. It would be their word against mine and only make my position worse when they all stood together and later hated me for revealing them.

"Daria, go back to class," Maryam Madam said. Her lips were white.

Daria hesitated. She said, "But the special lessons in . . ." and then saw enough in Maryam Madam's face to run out of the room.

"Why did you do that?" Naseema Madam asked, but Maryam Madam didn't answer. She went to the door and locked it, and then returned to her chair. She intertwined her fingers to rest her chin on them.

"Maryam?"

"You don't always need evidence to know what's true,"

Maryam Madam said without looking up. "You just need to be willing to get your head out of the sand."

"You're saying you believe—"

"I'm saying we'd be stupid to think that our girls are as innocent as we'd like them to be," Maryam Madam said, getting up and looking out her window. There wasn't anything to see but the ten-foot brick wall that held us in. "You think I need video footage to know that Leena and Aisha have been up to something? It's written all over their faces. And Mishail's grades wouldn't have dropped this much if she wasn't somehow still involved with that boy. These girls think they're so smart, but as you can see, they can't even control their tempers to save their lives."

I bit the inside of my cheek. I had never heard so much disappointment in Maryam Madam's voice. I wondered if she knew how each thing she said stung me deeper than the last. She knew about our *shillah*, or at least knew enough to not bother knowing more. Could Mishail really still be involved with Ahmed? True, he and I had been spending fewer nights together, but he'd always given me a good reason. *We're making the really dangerous part of the plan, best you don't know any more in case you're questioned. I don't know if I can stay away from temptation tonight, maybe it's best we don't see each other for a little while. I don't want to get in the way of your studies for your preliminaries.*

Suspicion clouded my thoughts until I could barely feel the rest of Maryam Madam's disappointment in me for losing my temper. How would I find out if there was still something between Mishail and Ahmed? And how would I stand it if it was true? Already my bones were rattling with nearly unbearable grief.

I came back to where we were when Aisha pinched my leg. Maryam Madam had just asked me a question over her shoulder. I blinked.

"I asked if you and Aisha were taking private lessons. I agree with Naseema that it wouldn't be Islamic to make something like that available to only some students but not all."

I glanced at Aisha. She spoke for the first time, saying, "Leena hasn't been taking any lessons, ma'am. But I have. From Leena."

"You've been *teaching* law?" Naseema Madam asked, sounding stunned.

I spoke to Maryam Madam's back. "I realized I had to take care of my own future," I said, hoping she felt as hurt by my words as I had by hers. "I've been reading cases from my father's practice, working with his partner when he can afford to pay me, and studying with Aisha. If *Daria* wants to share in that instead of spending her evenings flirting with the boys she picks up at Faisaliyah, she's *welcome* to join us."

Maryam Madam didn't turn to look at me, but her shoulders pinched upward, so I knew my words had found their mark.

"Leave us," she said. "Naseema and I need to talk."

Aisha and I didn't need to be told twice. We got out quickly. On the way back, Aisha dragged my sleeve, and we went to the bathroom and climbed up on the ledge. I was glad she'd thought of it, because I needed the fresh air.

"How do you do that?" Aisha asked eventually.

"Do what?"

"Be so brave. Say what you think without being afraid. It's what they've been trying to get me to do in the debate preparations, but I just freeze up when I'm talking to people. I get really soft and forget everything I know. But you! How do you stay so sharp? That, too, in front of *two* headmistresses!"

For the first time the word didn't make me angry. I *was* sharp, not a *garawiyya* who got fooled easily or who turned into a puddle in front of powerful people.

"They're just women," I said, feeling almost sad about it. "What's the worst they can do?"

18

SHABAB

Ahmed was in ecstasy! Whatever it was that he and the others had been waiting for, they'd found it. I could tell just from the way he drove when he picked me up.

Coca-Cola was right to call it dancing, what they did. See, one way to understand what cars meant to a Saudi was to listen to the Rowdha Yousefs of the world, the ones who insisted on their right to be chauffeured around by their guardians. It was only when I learned to drive, when the wind roared in my ears as I took the car all the way to 140 on the highway without even a prick of fear, that I understood what those women were so panicked about. Driving in Saudi Arabia wasn't about *transportation* or the practical question of getting from one point to another. Living in motion called to our blood as it did to our nomadic ancestors.

To us, driving wasn't about taming the land but about becoming one with its wildness. It was about power, a rite of passage to be taken with the utmost seriousness.

Ahmed's long fingers on the steering wheel were precise and determined as we drove out to the whiteland in the southern part of the city, the empty lots that were never built over because of the rancid industrial smoke-smell from the refineries.

"So what's the plan?" I asked.

"It's best you don't know the details. Don't you trust me? These things can get ugly. It's best if you don't get too mixed up in it."

I scowled and turned away. I hated how he talked about the things he'd decided were "best" for me, that he still treated me like a kid. I hated how needy I became when he did, and I hated that a part of me loved him more for trying to protect me. Above all, I hated the gnawing suspicion that he saw me only as a little sister, while his heart really belonged to Mishail.

"Don't sulk," he said. "Tonight we're celebrating."

"I'd celebrate more if I knew what we were celebrating."

He laughed and reached over to squeeze my hand in his. He let it go slowly, in a caress full of unmistakable intent.

"Oh, Leena, I love how you can always make me laugh. It won't be much longer now."

That kind of thing used to make me melt, but I realized only now, and with a sinking heart, that it was never what I actually wanted it to be. Never *I love you*.

I fought back the tears that threatened to spill. I told myself to be grateful that I had even this, the chance to feel love even if it wasn't returned. Most girls never felt anything this deeply, never in their lives knew a stronger love than for the posters of actors. Most of us had resigned ourselves to the thought that we'd grow up to be a kind of Fatima Aunty, a fat and gossiping crone who had several opinions but no passions.

"Here," Ahmed said in that fond tone he used when he knew I was upset about something. He pulled over, got out of the car, and came over to my side. "Why don't you drive?"

I shook my head and laughed. "You think that's all it takes to change my mood? I should increase my going rate. Start demanding Swarovski."

"It's no use, *habibti*," he said, and my heart skipped a beat at the casual way he dropped that endearment. "I know what you really want."

He was right. I loved driving, and I loved Ahmed's *shabab* with more fire and fury than I'd ever loved anything or anyone, including Ahmed himself. I loved the word itself, *shabab*. It meant a group of young men, but it sounded effervescent, like an explosion of youth and vigor. I loved how the car moved to meet my slightest wish as we raced down the shining roads with their perfect palm trees. I loved to listen to Coca-Cola in the car ahead lean out and scream his restlessness, his *tufshan*, as he drank in the dust-scented rain. I loved our music playing on the radio, and our poetry, which was the knife with which we carved our hopes into the rose sandstone of the Najd plateau.

Suddenly, Ahmed started swearing loudly, a string of curses so obscene it made me shudder to hear him.

In the distance, I heard sirens.

"How far away are they?" I asked. "Tell me where they are."

Ahmed turned to sit sideways, facing my profile. The police cars following us were several hundred feet away. He called out the distance and the road they were on, and I knew there was no way for us to stop and switch drivers. If we were caught, we'd go to jail, or worse if they found out I was a woman.

"We have to stop!" Ahmed shouted. "If we switch quickly, I can get us out of here!"

"There isn't time!" I said.

To my surprise, the simplicity of the situation made me calm. There was no choice but to get away, to do whatever it took to escape. I recalled my mental map of the city and said, "They've probably guessed we're going to Dirab Road, so maybe we can confuse them by getting on Ring Road and going east. Unless you have a better idea?"

When Ahmed said nothing, I snatched a look at him.

He looked furious and frightened, and I turned back to the road. We sped past an eternity of golden roads punctuated by car showrooms, McDonald's, and Euromarchés. We had long since overtaken Coca-Cola, who had disappeared into an alley.

Few other cars were on the highway this late at night. Once Ramadan was over and the shops had closed, there was nowhere left to go, and anyone still out this late moved hastily aside at the sound of the sirens.

An idea occurred to me. A mad one, but it was something. You could drive on Ring Road forever until you ran out of gas. Ahmed had done that on one of the other occasions. It was a wide, multilane loop around the city with a belt in the middle that allowed figure eights. But there was one place in the east, sandwiched between King Abdulaziz Hospital and the slums of Naseem, where Ring Road ended abruptly, hitting an intersection that would require a tight U-turn to put us right back on the highway going in the opposite direction.

"I'm going to Ali Al-Arini," I said. "I'll get off the highway—"

"And turn around," Ahmed said. "You're as mad as your father."

I grinned.

The car roared as if preparing to take flight. I held my breath as we came to the ramp. There was no traffic, so it was entirely down to skill. The car screeched and skidded as it slowed, but it obeyed me as if it were an extension of my body. I guided it around the turn and accelerated evenly on the curve back up onto the highway, hiding in plain sight.

The police cars got off the ramp and sped in the opposite direction.

We were free!

"I'm definitely ready to celebrate now!" I laughed aloud, my heart ready to burst with joy.

"Enough showing off," Ahmed said sharply. "We're late to meet the others."

I was so stung the car swerved, and Ahmed cursed again. I told myself to ignore it. He was just recovering from the stress of it all. He'd never have spoken to me like that otherwise.

"I don't think it's safe for you to be driving anymore," he said.

I nodded dumbly. Did he mean later tonight? Or forever? What was going through his mind, and why wouldn't he tell me?

We headed to an empty construction site to meet the *shabab*. The others were waiting for us, and when we arrived, the boys whooped and hollered out congratulations, hugging and kissing Ahmed as if he'd scored a winning goal. My mind was still on our fight, so it took me a moment to remember that we had come to talk about the rebellion.

"Speech!"

"Speech!"

"Tell us everything!"

Ahmed put his hands out to silence the crowd, as if to remind them that what we were doing was already illegal, as more than four people out after the *isha* prayer discussing politics was a crime. I thought with another thrill coursing through me that we had already got away with so much, broken so many laws in just the last hour.

Ahmed strode to the center of the space with a bounce in his step that was stunningly familiar.

"Tonight!" Ahmed said, and looked around the room. "Tonight we begin to take our vengeance!"

More cheers erupted. Someone groaned as if that were too far away.

"I know," Ahmed said, looking in that direction. "I know some of us have been waiting *years* for this. Long, painful years. And we know, don't we? How slowly time passes in the desert? How slowly time passes for those who know grief?"

He spoke with confidence, always meeting our eyes, and I realized he had practiced this moment. I had seen my father do this, control the room, pace his words, tell his story with both the command of a sheikh and the humility of a servant, as if reminding us that in the end it wasn't money or *wasta* that had allowed Muhammad to conquer the hearts of Mecca and Medina.

Words alone had won the two holy mosques.

"Let us remember the *hadith* of Al-Bayhaqi. *Whoever looks into the house of another without their permission, they may put out his eye with a stone without incurring sin.* Do our rulers and government ministers live by this? Do they not watch our houses, listen to our private conversations, and demand to know even our most private thoughts?"

There were loud, angry cheers, and once again Ahmed calmed down the crowd.

"Do they not try to turn us against one another, brother against brother, an Ahmed into a Fatullah, through threats and torture when *baksheesh* fails to corrupt us?"

The angry murmurs grew louder, and my heart started pounding in my ears. Even knowing that Ahmed was simply using the arts he had learned from my father didn't change the fact that those arts called for my blood to rise. My fists were clenched at my sides.

"But we will not betray one another, will we?"

"*No!*"

"Never!" I cried. Ahmed's eyes met mine, and for a moment, for one mad and jubilant moment, I *knew* we were alive with every cell of our being. I knew that I was in love beyond the call of reason or religion. I knew that if Ahmed asked me tonight, my answer would be yes.

"We will fight fire with fire!" Ahmed declared, and cheers erupted, so loud that I almost missed what he said afterward. Almost. "The minister who betrayed Hadi Mutazil will see that he isn't beyond our reach!"

I froze in shock as the other boys swarmed Ahmed to hug him and lift him into the air.

I told myself I'd misheard. Or that he could have meant any old minister. There were hundreds, after all.

How many could have betrayed your father, you idiot? You really think the mahabith *would have caught the most influential rebel in the country if it hadn't had help? How did Mishail's father go from rebel to interior minister in just a few short years?*

You just need to be willing to get your head out of the sand.

But what did Ahmed mean, the minister wasn't beyond his reach? Had Ahmed and Mishail worked out a plan together? Maybe Mishail had finally succeeded in finding something to blackmail the minister with, something that wasn't stupid statistics about youth delinquency.

I schooled my face into a mask of excitement on the drive back. It was easy enough, given that Ahmed was driving.

"How did you find out?" I asked, keeping my tone casual. "That the minister betrayed my father?"

"Mishail, of course," Ahmed said, and I didn't let myself flinch. She had never once told me.

"And she has the evidence? To use against her father?"

Ahmed laughed and muttered, "She *is* the evidence."

"What do you mean?"

"Nothing," Ahmed said, putting his arm around my shoulders. "As I said, trust me. That monster will see what it means to hurt us. He'll know what it feels like to have your family violated. I myself made sure of it."

Unease coiled in my gut, but I knew I couldn't let it show. I knew that other girls would probably be jealous of me now, that I had found a boy who loved me so much he would take my greatest burden from me. But I couldn't just say *Insh'allah* and hope for the best. I'd done it before out of laziness, sometimes out of fear, because that is what we women did, trusted our God and our guardians and never ourselves, and then complained when things didn't go our way.

I realized something, a simple thought that changed everything.

"The plan was always to get vengeance on Quraysh, wasn't it?" I asked meekly. "Not getting my father out?"

"Your father can come out any time he wants," Ahmed said with a casual shrug. "But only we can hurt the minister where he's weakest."

I nodded as if I had learned a great lesson. And maybe I had. It was suddenly clear to me that he had never once said that the plan was to get my father out of jail. I had assumed that, had let my hopes sit in the bag of his ambitions when he'd never had any intention of helping me at all. Not the way I wanted.

I studied his profile, wondering what I'd missed to have made such a great mistake in judgment. Was there something weak about his chin that I should have recognized? How could I have known that all he cared for was vengeance?

Daria, a voice whispered in my head. *Daria is how you knew.*

They were twisted in the same way, Ahmed and Daria, into thinking that destroying another person's happiness was the same thing as being happy. After enough unhappiness, it was easy enough to believe that the moments when the stick landed on others were the same thing as paradise.

I had to find out what Ahmed meant when he said that he was going after the minister where he was weakest. I had a suspicion, and so I said, "Do you need any help? With the minister, I mean. I could ask Mishail."

"No, it's already done. She gave me everything I needed. I'm not putting you at risk. Your father would never forgive me."

A plan formed in my mind. I said, "But you took a photo of me. How is that not putting me at risk?"

"You asked me to do that! But thanks for reminding me. It's probably best you delete that from your phone. Here"—he handed me his phone, as I'd hoped he would—"get rid of it from mine, too."

While he drove, I quickly searched through the photos. Not just for the one I knew he had taken of me, which I promptly deleted, but through his entire collection. I would recognize Mishail in a heartbeat.

"Your phone is really different from mine," I said to buy some time. "All the buttons are in different places."

I was just starting to doubt myself, to feel ashamed of my suspicions, when I saw it. The rays of dawn slicing through an east-facing window made of ornate wooden lattice, cut into a wall the color of coral.

I deleted it quickly, but I suspected that wasn't the end of it. I tried to think of what I might do if I had something truly incriminating on the minister's daughter. The answer was obvious. I found it then. A photo of Mishail, unveiled, smiling, her head against the pillow as if murmuring a secret.

Along with the photo of her bedroom window, this one was posted online for everyone to comment on.

For everyone on the Internet to know that the minister's daughter was unchaste.

"Still looking for it?" Ahmed said, and I fought down the flinch.

"Only just found the photos," I said, hoping my voice was calm.

How could he? How could he have kept this from me? Obviously Mishail had known he was taking this photo, because her eyes were open. Had she *wanted* him to use it? And if she hadn't, why would Ahmed believe that I would enjoy seeing my best friend humiliated publicly, for *any* reason?

I deleted the post, although the damage had probably already been done. I knew he'd find out soon enough, as soon as he got home or checked his phone again. When he did, he'd be furious, and he'd never speak to me again.

A wave of something almost like relief washed over me.

I handed the phone back to Ahmed, glad that it was dark and that he could see only my profile. We were only five blocks from my house. I just had to hold myself together until then.

"It was really smart of you to remember that," Ahmed said. His arm was still around my shoulder, and his fingers played with my hair. I wondered why he thought I was smart, wondered if he could feel my swallowing down my disgust, if he sensed the rapid pulse in my neck.

"*Sabah ul-khair*," he said as he dropped me off, his head jerking toward the sunrise. *Good morning.*

I got out of the car and waited until he had driven away before running into an alley. I leaned against the wall and sank to the ground, putting my head between my legs.

I couldn't move for a long time.

19

HUZUN

Before Ahmed, before Mishail, even, I had known a deep, transforming love. I had discovered it by accident, when I had cut myself with an X-ACTO knife I was using for an art project. Blood had come pounding out of my skin, unexpected and rich as an oasis in the desert. I'd recognized my love for what it was in those days after my father's arrest, when everything tasted like sand and time lost all meaning. It was why I'd taken the knife to my arms in the school bathroom.

Despite what Maryam Madam might have thought, I wasn't going to kill myself. I was just in love with pain, with that electric twang that started in my chest and ripped through my limbs until my palms twitched and reminded me that I was alive. Now, it coursed through me as a nearly blissful fury, leaving me light-headed and loose-limbed as I walked down the street. I knew I should go home. My mother would soon be awake, if she wasn't already. She sometimes rose with the dawn for the *fajr* prayer, getting up from her meditative state and shouting to me to wake up and get to school. On many days I never even saw her, just heard her calling from the kitchen, reminding me to do something or not to do something else.

It was a strange experience to be in such profound pain and yet still apparently whole, not bleeding out as if I'd been shot or ripped to shreds. I wished for that simpler, more comprehensible pain. At the very least, then nobody would think it strange if I started screaming.

"You there! Where are you going?" asked a voice behind me. I turned to look but didn't answer. The voice came from the passenger seat of an SUV. I blinked, unable to form any words. The car came to a stop a few feet away from me.

"I said, where are you going? The mosque is the other way."

With difficulty, I opened my mouth to say, "Walking." I couldn't really say any more than that. I didn't actually recognize where I was. I had no idea what time it was or how long I'd been walking.

"Are you trying to be smart with us? Who are you?"

I could've started running. I seemed to be on some

wide boulevard with vapid sunflowers gaping at me from white bungalows, but if I ran far enough, I would have reached Haara or Batha or some other district where a car would have been unable to follow and where I could have outrun any old *muttawa*.

But I didn't feel real. I was floating. I was a cloud that shifted around my body rather than a solid contained within it. My legs refused to move. My mouth refused to work.

"Show us your ID!" the man cried, getting out of the car and marching toward me.

Still, I said nothing. I wanted to say I didn't have my ID on me, but words slipped from my grasp like sand. He grasped my collar and shoved me against a wall, leaning close to my face. I made a startled sound and saw that he'd realized I was a woman. He cursed and jumped back, wiping his hands and spitting as if he had touched something polluted. The *muttaween*, these members of Al-Hai'a, the Committee for the Propagation of Virtue and Prevention of Vice, were supposed to be the pinnacle of chastity. They did not even speak to women, only ever directed their guardians to scold their womenfolk when their veils weren't properly fastened.

And this guy had just realized he had touched a woman and had pressed himself up against her enough to know for sure.

I shouldn't have, but I couldn't help myself. I laughed. The *muttawa* pulled out his stick and landed three blows on my arms and legs before I could make myself stop. He hit me repeatedly until I moved as he wanted toward the SUV. His partner had left the driver's seat and was opening the back door for me. If he hadn't been glowering at me, I would have thought he was some kind of limousine driver taking me to a party.

Sitting in the back, I was glad of the pain in my arms and legs. It was distracting, and it took my mind off the fact that Ahmed had been in Mishail's bedroom. It didn't really matter what had or hadn't happened between them. Even if all they had done was sit on opposite sides of the room, even if she had remained fully veiled, even if they had never touched each other, they had shared a secret I hadn't known. I was the innocent, ignorant one. I understood now that love, not the *niqab*, was the real veil over our eyes, that hope and not the *abaya* was the cage in which we were imprisoned. Love and hope drove us to wait in silence to be rescued from our fates.

The *muttaween* took me to the station. I don't know why, but I'd expected a jail cell with bars on the windows and a one-way mirror, the kind they had on television shows. Instead, it was almost like waiting to see the doctor at the National Hospital, a clean room that smelled a little too much of disinfectant, full of bored people trying not to fall asleep. Someone screamed in the distance, either from being tortured or from waiting in the emergency room with a broken arm, I couldn't tell the difference.

A fully veiled woman came forth to escort me to a

questioning room. When we were alone, the woman unveiled and asked me who I was, as if I hadn't answered the *muttawa* because he was a man.

"Please phone Maryam Alkhalaf," I said. I mentioned her relationship to the Sudairi family and watched the woman's eyes grow wide. "My name is Leena. Her son is my guardian."

I was quickly transported to yet another room, one more in line with my imagination. A small, ragged carpet in the corner was left for me to pray on. The rest of the room was covered in linoleum and smelled too clean, that disinfectant smell that meant people had left bodily fluids of one kind or another on the tarpaulin.

I paced the room, letting my fingers run across the brick walls. Eventually the female guard who had questioned me entered and dragged me out by the elbow. I wondered idly if this was what jail was like for women, a bureaucratic nightmare of being led from one windowless room to another, waiting for paperwork to be stamped, and eventually discovering that the obscure rules intended to empower women were now being used to imprison them. Wasn't that the way life worked? Muhammad had abolished the right of the hand, forbidding men to take more than four of us for their possession. It was his great negotiation, intended to help women who were slaves and concubines, to help widows of a war-torn desert, a compromise welcomed until we discovered that other women, elsewhere, could have the whole of a man's heart to themselves and none of his fists.

My thoughts ran on until I was taken to yet another room covered in linoleum, this one looking like one of those in-home beauty salons that the Palestinian and Yemeni women set up to make money, using homemade *halawa* or sugar wax, to give us unevenly smooth legs that nobody would ever see.

An old crone who had been dozing in a chair smiled toothlessly at me, giddy with the prospect of a customer.

"You rich kids," the guard said, "you think you can get away with anything. No consequences."

"I'm not rich," I said.

"Not rich, huh?" the guard repeated sarcastically. "You think the women piled in the hovels of Naseem are phoning Sudairis before breakfast?" She dragged me to a chair. There was a strange brownish-black dust on the floor, and I realized with horror what it was: human hair.

"No!"

"*Be quiet!* And be glad that's all we're cutting off!"

My blood ran cold. I had heard the stories of women, usually wild foreign women, who were captured for indecency and underwent something known only as *khassa*, the cutting. . . . a procedure that tamed them for work in the harems in Bahrain. I didn't know what it involved and didn't want to.

"First time?" asked the wrinkled crone. She held an

electric shaver in her hand. "Come, come. It'll grow back soon."

I tried to break free of the guard's grip, only to receive a hard slap.

"Hold still or you'll get hurt."

The guard shoved me into the chair and placed her knee on my thigh. I tried to throw her off, but the weight was too much. My muscles weren't cooperating. Meanwhile, the crone had started shaving my head.

This was the standard punishment, the most lenient one, for feminine indecency.

The buzzing sent shudders down my spine. I felt rather than heard my hair fall. It had never been very long, but I had finally been ready to grow it out, to stop looking like a boy now that I knew what I could look like with my hair blowing behind me in the wind as I drove.

I closed my eyes and prayed quietly. I didn't have the strength to look in the mirror in front of me. I felt hollow, as if the last of my tethers had been taken and I was falling into a bottomless abyss.

"Get up," the guard said. "Your guardian is here."

I opened my eyes and saw myself in the mirror. I couldn't even recognize the face in front of me, red eyes blazing out of sunken cheeks, a bluish-white head shaped like a dented fruit.

The horror had just begun. I had to face Maryam Madam, my mother, my friends at school. I could avoid Ahmed, but no one else.

The world of women would bear witness to my shame. I knew I'd *said* I could live by the words of the rebels, I'd claimed that I would pay any price for freedom, suffer any consequences for what I believed. But I was sixteen, and my one and only vanity had turned to dust on a sticky floor.

I swayed on my feet as the guard dragged me to the headmistress.

"This one?" she asked, as if I were a chicken being picked out of a cage.

Maryam Madam nodded. Her lips were white, so I knew she was furious.

"We're *so* sorry," the guard said, sounding truly contrite. "We had *no idea* she was special. We had followed the procedure before she even told us who she was and asked us to call you."

Anger made me snap my arm free. I was about to say something when I saw the headmistress widen her eyes in warning. Her head shook only a fraction, but I saw it and silenced my tongue.

"*Illi faat mat,*" Maryam Madam said with a smile, placing a hand gently on the guard's shoulder. It meant, *What's past is dead.* "You were only doing your duty, dear."

The guard stood stupidly, struck dumb by the headmistress's gentle tone. I realized what she'd expected: the casual cruelty we'd come to expect from the rich and infamous.

"When can I take her home?" Maryam Madam asked.

"Let me check for you, ma'am," the guard said, veiling herself and entering the main lobby, where the men's offices were. She left Maryam Madam and me staring at each other in silence.

"You win more friends with honey," Maryam Madam said.

I knew I ought to say something—*sorry, thank you, I didn't do anything wrong*—but all I could think of was "Isn't it time for school?"

"It is," Maryam Madam said. "Naseema can take care of things."

Then she leaned in for a hug. I startled away for a half second before I let her hold me.

"What have you told them?" she whispered in my ear. "What were you doing? Do they know whose daughter you are?"

"Only that my name is Leena," I said. "I wasn't doing anything. Just walking. Alone."

"Good," Maryam Madam said, stepping away. I missed her warmth instantly, and her delicate rose perfume.

The guard returned, looking flustered. "I'm sorry, ma'am, but the report here says that she insulted a *muttawa* and touched him inappropriately."

I squawked in surprise, but Maryam Madam touched the back of my arm to get me to be quiet.

"We need a promise from her guardian that he'll keep her in check before we can let her go."

"My son is her guardian," Maryam Madam said. "He's at school. Isn't it enough for us to sign?"

"Sorry, ma'am. He has to come in and identify himself for it to be official."

I saw Maryam Madam's jaw clench and then release. When she spoke, her eyelashes batted almost flirtatiously. "Is it enough if the signature comes from a government official?"

"As long as it's from a man who agrees to take responsibility for her behavior in the future," the guard said, looking embarrassed.

Maryam Madam smiled. My heart raced because I knew what she was going to do, and I couldn't bear to let her do it. I couldn't be in the debt of the man who had betrayed my father, the man who was responsible for my unfortunate situation in the first place. I wouldn't let myself be humiliated by groveling up to the minister for a favor. I wouldn't let anyone from that family of traitors help me.

"No!" I shouted, surprised at the hatred in my voice. "My father is Hadi Mutazil. Call him! Tell him I'm here."

"Leena, *no!*"

The guard looked between us uncertainly.

I shook my head. "They want my father to come home? This is the way. Tell him I'm in jail. Tell him to sign the *taahud* and come from his jail to this one, and then sign my *taahud*."

Tears flowed down my cheeks. I couldn't stop them.

"Leena, be quiet!"

I folded my arms around my chest.

"Is it true?" the guard asked, looking as stunned as if she'd seen a unicorn. "This is the rebel's daughter?"

"No," Maryam Madam said.

"Yes," I said.

The guard ran back out to the lobby.

"What did you do that for?" Maryam Madam hissed.

"They said there was only one way to make him come home," I muttered through my sobs. "Only one woman who could make him come home. I just want him to come home."

"Who said?"

"Please," I said, and the rest of my words tumbled out before I could stop them, "my mother's planning to get a divorce."

Another electric shock of pain ripped through my body.

"Oh, Leena," Maryam Madam said. I shook my head and turned away. I didn't want her sympathy. I was sick of everyone's *zakat*, their charity and pity and kindness. I just wanted the world to be fair for one damned minute.

"Leena, there's something you should know," Maryam Madam said, taking her hands in mine. "You know that I love you as if you were my own daughter, don't you?"

I nodded. I wouldn't have called her if I hadn't known it.

"When your father was arrested, I promised him I'd

take care of you no matter what. You would never have to worry about school fees, uniforms, textbooks, going to college, none of that."

I looked at her in surprise. I had assumed that my mother's catering business had paid for all that.

She leaned in to whisper, "Your father *chose* this. He's far more powerful as a symbol of resistance than he would be out here, under surveillance. They *planned* this, your father and Karim. He won't come home."

I shook my head dumbly. I couldn't believe it. No man would decide to put his family at risk to play out some Raif Badawi fantasy, staying in jail purely to stir up a national rebellion. It had to be a lie. And Karim? How could the headmistress speak the minister's first name so casually, as if they were friends? He was a monster who had destroyed someone else's family to enrich his own, a sniveling, bootlicking traitor in search of power.

The female guard entered, her face white. She said, "Put on your veils. The minister's on his way."

20

ITJIHAD

We waited, silent and veiled, while the minister snapped at the guards and signed some paperwork that we weren't allowed to see.

"*Yellah*," he said, and marched out without waiting for us. Maryam Madam grabbed my arm and followed him.

"My driver's waiting," Maryam Madam said.

"Get Norah, leave her, meet me at the usual place."

Norah. My mother. My blood boiled at the way he used her name, as if he had the right. But he was gone before I could speak, his gait so crisp and quick that his shoes tapped down the long staircase like a hammer.

I got into the back of a Chevrolet that had a curtain between us and the driver. Maryam Madam instructed him to take us to my house. So she knew where it was.

None of this made any sense. Not unless Maryam Madam was telling the truth. I tried to remember the night of my father's arrest, but it was a blur. My mother was screaming for them to stop. My father was screaming that it would all be fine. *Insh'allah.* Even in that moment, he'd remembered to ensure his promises about the future with the mercy of God, as if knowing that he could do nothing alone.

If it was true, then the minister was one of us. But what did that mean, really, one of *us*?

If it was true, and if the wrong people found out, death would be a kindness compared with what those in power would do to us all.

The car stopped in front of my house. I wondered if my mother would be there and hoped desperately that she wouldn't. I didn't want to face her. I wanted to stay in the car, hidden behind black silk forever.

"I called her," Maryam Madam said. "She knows. I told her to wait. I said I'd bring you back."

I swallowed.

"Tell her Yasin Al-Mudathir is angry that the lunch he ordered has not yet arrived. Can you remember that? She'll come right down if you do. Tell her nothing else."

I shook my head. "No."

"What do you mean, no? Yasin Al-Mudathir. It's an easy name."

"*No,*" I said, digging my fingernails into my thigh. "I won't stay in the dark anymore. I want to know what's going on. Who's Yasin Al-Mudathir? Where are we meeting him? What does he want?"

Maryam Madam looked nervously toward the driver. Of course he was listening. Everyone was always listening. As if I didn't know that the reason I couldn't even talk to my own mother was that our house was under surveillance. Our phones were under surveillance.

"Look, there's no reason for you to get involved in—"

"*No reason?*" I snarled, pointing at my shorn scalp peeking out from under the veil. "I'm already involved! I'm the one who has to suffer the consequences of every decision you make!"

Maryam Madam drew a sharp breath.

"I'll get her," I said. "But I'm coming with you."

I leaped up the steps to my house two at a time. It was when I got to the door that I realized that Yasin and Al-Mudathir were the other names of the prophet Muhammad. Al-Mudathir meant *the one who is concealed*.

My mother opened the door and pulled me into a hug. I felt cold, disconnected from her.

I spoke my piece to her as I'd been instructed. She nodded and pulled away, grabbing her *abaya* and her keys. She was about to close the door when she realized I was with her on the outside.

"I'm coming," I said.

She wouldn't look at me, but she locked the door and didn't argue. Her eyes were red from crying. We went down to the car and drove in a tense silence to Suleimaniya Park.

In the winter months, the desert wind was laced with fog and dust, cool and moist as a kiss. In the summer, the air conditioners in cars tried to mimic that but usually went overboard, blasting dust in your face until you coughed, and then sending out five thin streams of cold air that covered only one half of your body while the other half baked in sunlight coming through the windows.

Suleimaniya Park was to a real park what air-conditioning was to an Arab who had tasted the winter wind. White fluorescent lights shone too brightly at night, and now, during the day, hung their heavy heads in slumber every thirty feet. Candy wrappers were strewn about the clearings, and Bangladeshi men in green jumpsuits unobtrusively picked them up with metal pincers. There were very few trees. The vast majority of the park was formed by tall, shiny hedges that formed a labyrinth. The hedges were manicured flat at the top and stood in neat rows, creating semiprivate spaces for families to have picnics (fully veiled, of course), as if the greenery around us had been fashioned into the stalls of a special kind of public toilet.

We sat down in one of these stalls, which seemed less used than the others. Maryam Madam had led us there without hesitation.

"He won't sign a divorce," Maryam Madam said suddenly. "You know that, don't you?"

My mother drew herself upright and glared at me.

"And you want me to play the martyr wife," my mother

said. "You want me to cry in front of news reporters and beg for his release, when all he ever had to do was sign a paper to come home?"

I realized from the anger in her voice that she hadn't known about the *taahud*. So she'd been just as shocked and betrayed as I'd been. *That* was when things had started. When she cried at Hossein's office. When the minister had confronted me in the hallway and said *he won't sign*. That was when she'd started preparing for a divorce.

I couldn't blame her.

"He can't sign," the minister said in a low voice from the clearing next to ours. "Not now. If *he* submits, nobody else will dare rise up again. That's always been our problem before, low numbers. We need him."

I bent my head to hide my bitterness. It was fine for him to secretly be one of the rebels, while he enjoyed all the benefits that came from siding with the authorities.

Still, he was right about the low numbers of the rebels. When Manal Al-Sharif organized her Facebook revolution, asking women to drive in protest of the law, to at least be able to drive to a hospital in case of an emergency, half a million people watched the video, but only a few dozen came out to support her. Even other *women* called her a pot-stirrer, a troublemaker, someone who was setting back the reformers' negotiations with her impatience.

Why aren't more of us out there? I'd asked Mishail once, when my frustration had found no outlet for weeks.

Manal can't do what you can, she'd replied, as if that was any kind of an answer.

"How is that my problem?" my mother said. "I don't care about your revolution or your conspiracies. I just want—"

She broke off and looked away, swallowing. "What do you want?" Maryam Madam asked, placing a hand on my mother's cheek.

My mother shoved it away. "Don't you dare offer your sympathy, you damned concubine!"

Maryam Madam nursed her hand as if it had been slashed with a knife. She said nothing. I wondered how she could stay so calm. My face was hot with shame that my mother had even used such an ugly word.

"You might as well know, Leena," my mother said when the silence drew on, "unless you thought it was an easy matter for her son, Shoaib, to become your guardian. I wondered how you did that, Maryam, since I'd been struggling to make Faraz her *wali*, but they wouldn't allow it. He wasn't related in any way. But two weeks of paperwork from you and some random child gets to be my daughter's guardian? You didn't even have to tell me, never mind *ask* me first."

"It's not like that," Maryam Madam said, her face now as red as mine felt. "We were just friends, but it's not legal for a man and a woman to be friends in this country, so we wrote up a contract. That's all."

223

"Enough," said the minister, sounding as if he couldn't understand why any of this was even a problem for the women he couldn't see. "This isn't the time for this. I signed for Leena, saying I'd keep her out of trouble. Can you handle that, or do I need to do something?"

My mother looked at me, and her eyes took on a wild, calculating look, as if she couldn't believe the bargain she was being offered.

"I need permission to get Leena married, so she can be independent," she said quickly, and my jaw dropped. "It won't be a real marriage, *just a contract*." She sneered at Maryam Madam. "But she needs a real *wali*, a guardian who can actually represent her, not some child she hasn't met."

"She's *sixteen!*" Maryam Madam begged. "Why can't you just wait a little longer? We're working on reforms. Even this debate at the *Majlis* is such a monumental change. Do you think it could've happened if we hadn't been patient?"

"Your precious debate?" my mother said with a laugh. "Where you've got some reformers disguised as model citizens, so that maybe the *muttaween* will allow us to put designs and glitter on our *abayas*?"

"It doesn't matter anyway," the minister said. "She can't get married without her father's permission. You're right about one thing. Shoaib's guardianship is only for educational matters. He isn't a real *wali*."

"*Adhl*," I said suddenly. My mother glared at me, as if amazed I'd had the temerity to interrupt the adults' conversation. As if they hadn't been talking about me all along. As if this wasn't my *life* they were arguing about.

"What?"

"*Adhl*," I repeated. "If a *wali* doesn't permit the woman in his guardianship to marry according to her own choice, she can sue for *adhl* and find a new *wali* to support her."

I sent up a prayer of gratitude to Hossein and Faraz for all those years of law lessons.

"Even for *adhl*—" the minister said.

"You needed a *mahram*'s support, yes," I said, my heart racing. "But that law was changed three weeks ago. The state is guardian for women without a guardian. It's the same form that's used to give women permission to marry a non-Saudi, the permission from the king."

There was silence. I didn't really know why I was helping except that I knew my mother was right about one thing. I needed a *wali*, a guardian of my own choice, someone I could trust not just with my life but with my soul, someone who wasn't going to rot away in prison, gamble away our fortunes, or value vengeance over our survival.

"I know which one you mean," the minister said. "I'll have it signed and sent to your mother."

"To me, you mean," I said quietly, my eyes fixed on my mother. I saw a strange mix of anger and amusement in her eyes, but she didn't say anything.

"Fine," the minister said. There was a rustling sound, and then silence, so I knew he'd left.

"Norah, this is ridiculous," Maryam Madam said. "She's so young. Don't we agree at least that a girl shouldn't be married until she's eighteen? With a mind like hers, Leena ought to go to college. Won't you let me at least put in a word to—"

"You can put in all the words you like," my mother said, getting up and dusting off her black *abaya*. "After Leena has found herself a new *wali*. After that, you can take it up with him. *I* may be stuck with no say in my own affairs, but I'll die before I let my daughter suffer my fate."

The rest of the day passed in a blur. My mother said very little, but she made all my favorite dishes. Neither of us left the house. We turned on the TV and watched comedy shows together, drinking diluted laban filled with spices. The phone rang a lot, but my mother simply disconnected it when she realized it was Fatima Aunty calling. She had a strange look in her eyes, as if she was secretly happy about something.

"What?" I asked, retying my headscarf self-consciously. It kept sliding off, revealing the bald head I didn't want to see.

My mother shook her head.

Eventually I went to bed. I took off the headscarf and stared at my reflection. Tears filled my eyes, and I fell into bed, sobbing into my pillow. My chest felt as if someone were pinching my heart from the inside.

I'd been crying so long and hard that I hadn't heard the door open. My mother came to lie down beside me. I didn't move, so she enveloped me, throwing her arms around my shoulders and nuzzling her head into my neck.

"Leena, would you like me to tell you a story?"

I shrugged. I didn't care. As if any story were going to make me feel better. Tomorrow I'd have to go to school and face all my classmates. I wasn't going to be able to play this off with pride the way Mishail had done. I hadn't been caught for any glamorous crime, just for walking down the street dressed improperly. That was the worst part.

My mother said, "A long time ago there was a tribe that was passing through Wadi Al-Shafa by the Sarawat Mountains. To get through, the group had to climb long, hard days across the mountains with very little to eat. They had no shoes on their feet. There was a young girl among them, and she struggled to keep up with the others. The men kept telling her father, Abu Rihan, 'You are of the age where your sons should be bearing you up, but instead, you are bearing up your daughter. Your daughter is holding you back, and she'll be the death of us.'"

I made myself stop sobbing. It had been so long since I'd heard this version of my mother's voice, soft and soothing, not hollering commands.

"Abu Rihan loved his daughter, and so he carried her as far as he could. But he was an old man, and he moved slowly with the weight on his back, until the girl Rihan felt sorry and said, 'Leave me here. *Insh'allah* I'll live.' So the tribe left the girl behind. She smiled bravely and carried on as far as she could on her own, until one night, unable to see in the dark, she fell into a well. She didn't know how to swim, so she cried for help. A man heard her. This man, Nabil, was a poet who would climb to the mountains at night to listen to the angels."

There was an urgency in my mother's voice now, a *do you understand?* that seeped through in her tone. I fell completely silent and tried to make sense of it. Nabil might just be a name, but it was also a rarely used word for a prophet, a herald.

"Nabil couldn't pull Rihan out of the well himself, so he threw a log into it for her to hold on to. He said he would find help in the city, and he left her there. He went down to the city of Al-Shafa and wrote long and beautiful poems about how the men of the mountains were wicked, leaving their women to die in wells. He issued a *fatwa* that any man who left a woman to die when he could save her would burn in hell. But the people of Al-Shafa stoned him, and so he ran to Yathrib and never returned to save Rihan."

I knew now that this was no ordinary story. Yathrib was the original name for Madinah Al-Munawwarah, the second-holiest city in our world. The prophet Muhammad used to climb the Sarawat Mountains around Mecca at night. It was where he heard the angel Jibrail. The verses of the Quran had come to him, and he'd spoken against the corruption in Mecca. He'd been chased out, and he ran to Yathrib in the *hijra*. My mother was telling me a religious story, but in the only way she could in our country, where heresy and apostasy could be punished by death.

She continued, "But the men of Al-Shafa who had turned out Nabil now burned with the desire for glory. They were moved by the story of this beautiful woman trapped in a well, who had so bravely given herself to Allah's mercy, who waited to be rescued by one of them. Of all the young men, only Yasin dared climb the mountains that had killed so many. He had the skill of a mountain goat and the words of the poet Nabil to vouch for him. And he was beautiful, his falcon eyes spearing women and men with desire and envy."

My mother laughed, a delicate and fond sound, and my heart lurched toward her. I knew who she meant. I'd seen those eyes—my father's eyes—in the mirror.

"Yasin traveled the mountains in search of this courageous woman who had sacrificed herself so her father might live. He found her in the well, still holding on to the log, waiting for Nabil to return. He told her what had happened to Nabil and threw her a rope, but he wasn't strong enough to pull her out. So he left her hanging there by her shoulders, her feet in the well, her body cold and shivering. He said he knew a friend in Al-Shafa who worked for the government, who could arrange for a crane. With the crane's machinery, he wouldn't be able to just pull her out, but any woman who ever found herself in a well. So saying, he left for Al-Shafa. But it was Friday, so the government wouldn't let him borrow the crane, and he burned with fury over his impotence. He stood in the city center and cried out about the corrupt and lazy government that would let women hang in wells when there was no reason to abandon them there. The people got angry and threw him in prison."

This last was hushed. I turned to my side so I could see her face. My mother smiled at me and thumbed a tear from my cheek.

"A chance traveler came upon the well," she said. "He wondered why a woman hung half dead from a rope between earth and sky. Rihan had not eaten in days, her hair had turned the color of sand from being bleached by the sun, and her lips were so cracked she couldn't even ask for help. The traveler, Hassan, had very little to eat himself and was on his way to Al-Shafa. But he knew he couldn't leave her there. So he gave her all his food and water until Rihan could speak and move a little. He asked her to kick against the wall, to use her hands and feet to climb. He said he didn't have the strength to pull her up himself, but if she helped him, maybe they could manage it together. Rihan cried and said, 'I'm such a burden to everyone. Why don't you just cut the rope and let me die?' Hassan laughed and said, 'You just drank all my water. If you don't bring me some on your way up, we'll both die.' Knowing she was responsible for saving Hassan gave Rihan the strength and courage she had lost. She fought her way up, bringing him water to drink in her wet clothes. Together they stumbled to Al-Shafa. And what do you think Nabil and Yasin thought of this?"

I huffed a laugh into her neck.

"You know what I've learned, Leena?" she asked. Her voice sounded choked up, as if she were fighting back tears.

"Tell me."

"Don't marry the man who offers you a hand when you are drowning. Such men are always looking for more drowning women to save. Marry the one who teaches you to swim."

21

KALAM EN-NAS

I thought about making up stories. Plausible enough that they would require no evidence, but not so scandalous that they would horrify any listeners and get me into even more trouble.

One story was that I had been caught for letting my *abaya* hang open below the waist and wearing jeans and high heels that sprang out of the trailing black cape. It was the fashion in Jeddah these days to wear this sort of outfit and go for long walks on the boardwalk, with the rose-and-gold city to one side and the Red Sea on the other.

Another story was that I had fought with the *muttawa* and kicked him between the legs, and so even though I hadn't been doing anything terribly exciting I had at least put up a meaningful resistance.

This was the thing about life in Riyadh, this city of contradictions. As Mishail had once put it, you had to be totally modern and totally Islamic at the same time, open-minded, but not so much that your brains fell out. You had to turn into a creature as astute at politics as a royal princess while being so modest that nothing of it showed in your downcast eyes, someone who knew what was going on without being told, knew who did and did not matter, and above all knew how to manage *kalam en-nas*, what people would say.

It was the skill of Riyadh's street cats and its women, a survival instinct that was currently on high alert as I entered the classroom.

None of my stories were necessary, though. Aisha caught me as soon as I arrived and guided me to a seat next to her own.

"Why didn't you answer your phone yesterday?" she demanded. "I've been trying to reach you. I had to be the first to tell you what really happened before you heard any rumors."

"Tell me what?"

"It wasn't my fault. I mean it was, but it wasn't, you know?"

"No! What are you even talking about?"

"They all know," Aisha said, "about the driving."

"How?" I asked, my heart sinking.

"I didn't want to leave the photo you gave me at home. I have a very annoying younger brother who goes through all my stuff and shows what he finds to my parents. So I always kept your evidence in our law textbook and took it to school every day."

"*Aisha*," I groaned, knowing where this was headed.

"While I was in the bathroom, Bilquis and Daria found it in my bag. They wanted to know if I was using some secret way to prepare for the debate, and—"

"Wait, Bilquis and *Daria*?" I asked. How had that allegiance been formed, and so quickly? The most conservative and most liberal girls were friends now?

"They wanted to show Naseema Madam what was really going on in the school behind her back."

"Why?"

"Daria's just Daria; she's not happy unless someone else is in trouble," Aisha said, looking exasperated, as if all the questions I was asking her were about the introduction and she wanted to get on with telling the real story. "And I think Bilquis wants to replace me on the debate team now. She's got some new fire behind her engine."

As if we'd summoned her by saying her name, Bilquis appeared in front of us. Her arms were folded in front of her, and she stood over us like some kind of bodyguard.

"Has this one tried to sell you some story about how we went through her bag?" Bilquis asked. "Let me tell you what really happened. We got the news immediately that you'd been arrested. Naseema Madam is smart, not like that idiot Maryam. She knew the next step would likely be an investigation into the school. It's about time, really, if you ask me. But Naseema didn't know whom she could trust, so she asked a few of us to prepare the school for a *muttawa* raid and confiscate any forbidden materials. That's all."

"And you chose *my* bag first and last?" Aisha said. "How convenient."

"The other girls handed over their materials immediately, no questions," Bilquis said, tossing her hair. "Even Mishail."

At the name, I flinched, feeling sick to my stomach. I couldn't bring myself to think about her and Ahmed. I had stared at my phone a dozen times in the last day, aching to call one of them. But what if I called Mishail to confess my heartbreak and she told me it served me right? What if I told Ahmed what had happened and he said something that proved he wasn't in love with me after all?

It's fine, Leena. I always thought of you as one of the boys anyway.

I clutched at my stomach.

"What's wrong with you two?" Bilquis said. "Say *Leena* in front of Mishail, and she runs to the bathroom to vomit. Looks like you react the same way."

I frowned. *What?*

"Anyway, it should all be sorted out soon," Bilquis continued. "The trouble with the *muttaween* in this country is that they're all men, and so they think like men. To protect the virtue of a woman, you need to think like a woman. I've realized that's what I want to do with my life. I want to become the first woman *muttawa*, to help other women. To think in the curvy, mixed-up, secretive ways that women think and show them the straight path instead, bring them relief."

"I see," I said, struggling to keep a straight face.

"Anyway, that's why I'm here now, Leena. You and I, we've had our differences, but after what you've been through I know you're finally ready to return to the straight path. I know you need real friendship, not what *this one* is offering you, hiding your secrets so you can continue to be Leena Adhaleena. I just wanted to offer my forgiveness, and let you know that if you need guidance, I'm here to help."

I stared at Aisha, who was staring at Bilquis. How was I supposed to respond to that? A part of me wanted to spit in Bilquis's face or punch her, but the memory of Maryam Madam with the prison guard came to me, and I held back.

"They are truly lucky," I said carefully, "who can learn from the experience of others without having to make their own mistakes."

Bilquis beamed and walked away.

"What's wrong with you?" Aisha said. "You're turning into a *multazimat* now? She's the enemy!"

"No, she isn't," I said, feeling the truth of it down to my bones. "There's no us or them. There's just one *ummah*, and we're all in it, and we're never going to climb out of the well if we keep fighting each other over little things."

"What are you talking about? What well?"

"It doesn't matter," I said, shaking off my anger at Bilquis. What was the use of fighting with her when I had so many bigger problems? I asked Aisha, "What did she mean about Mishail?"

"She saw the photo, too. They passed it around. Most of the girls didn't even mind that you were driving, they just admired your sunglasses. Sofia said that after all, there's no law against women driving anymore; it was just that people didn't dare do it. But Mishail—she saw the photo, grabbed it from us, and stared at it as if there was some hidden secret. Then she ran to the bathroom and threw up. She cried all day, too, and wouldn't talk to any of us."

She must have guessed whose car I was in. Mishail hadn't arrived at school yet. I wondered if she would come or if she'd have her driver send in a sick note.

"And where's the photo now?" I asked.

"Naseema Madam took it. She said she and Maryam Madam would figure out what to do with all the confiscated materials, and that was the end of it. And Maryam

Madam never came back yesterday, so I don't know what happened next."

The door opened, and Mishail slipped inside, quiet and subdued. The whispers around her fell and then rose again. The way she looked at me tore me to bits. There was no accusation in her eyes, just loneliness, guilt, and despair.

And right then I knew beyond a shadow of a doubt that Ahmed hadn't told her the real reason he'd taken her photograph. He had always intended to use her in his plan for vengeance. He had never loved her, not for a minute. We had both been equally betrayed.

In a moment of madness, I walked right up to her and gathered her in a hug. She threw her arms around my neck and burst into tears.

I didn't care who was looking. I didn't care what anyone thought. Never mind *kalam en-nas*. There was one truth at the center of my existence that needed no evidence, and it was that I couldn't let Mishail be hurt on my watch.

"I didn't know," she whispered. "I saw his reflection in your sunglasses yesterday. I'd never have—"

"I found out what he did yesterday," I admitted, feeling a weight lift off my shoulders. "I deleted the post, but then I went crazy. I walked around. That's when they caught me."

The classroom door burst open, and Maryam Madam demanded I go with her immediately.

"We'll talk later," I promised.

"Nothing they do can touch us," Mishail promised back, smiling wanly.

"One day," Maryam Madam muttered as we walked down the hallway. "I was gone for one day. Is it too much to ask that we can go *one bloody day* without a crisis?"

She slammed open her office door and slammed it shut. Naseema Madam was inside, looking like a child who had caught her hand in a candy jar.

"These arrived for you today," Maryam Madam said, snapping a folder against the table.

I didn't have to see more than the Ministry of the Interior letterhead to know what it was. My freedom, signed and sealed, delivered as promised. I reached for the folder hungrily, and the headmistress snatched it away.

"You don't think I want you to have this?" she asked. "When I first met Norah, I thought she was an idiot. But this is a brilliant idea, I've got to hand it to her. I think of your career, she thinks of your husband. I think about education, she thinks about money. And *this*"—she waved the precious folder around—"could be the answer not just to your prayers but to so many girls' prayers. So I asked him to send me more than one. Five to start with, only to be used in emergencies. And I got in today and shared the great news with Naseema, and what do I hear?"

Maryam Madam paused, as if we were supposed to complete her thought. Naseema Madam squirmed uncomfortably.

"Un-Islamic, says my esteemed colleague," Maryam Madam finished. "Not illegal, mind you, which can be worked around, but un-Islamic. Because it has to be signed by two Muslims, and together she and I only count as one. Not a problem! I said I'd get Shoaib to sign as the other. That's when Naseema squirmed even more than she's doing right now and told me what was really bothering her. That there's something more that's required for a valid marriage that isn't covered in this document. Take a guess."

I didn't have to guess.

"Chastity," I muttered. "You need to assert our chastity."

Maryam Madam snapped her fingers in fury. "Exactly! Chastity. And that's when Naseema showed me something that made my heart stop. A photo. A *printed* photo of you driving around somewhere, wearing no veil, and acting like some idiotic Hollywood starlet. And who in the world was *taking* the photo? Neither of us has any idea. It could be a *mahram*. Or it could be that all this while I thought you, you of *all* my girls, knew the difference between freedom and stupidity, but I was wrong. Tell me, Leena, which is it?"

I smiled, batting my eyelashes as I'd seen Maryam Madam do at the prison guard yesterday.

"He's just a friend, ma'am. But it's not considered legal for a man and a woman to be friends in this country, is it?"

Maryam Madam stared at me for a half minute, and then threw back her head and laughed. She laughed so hard she doubled over and wiped tears from her eyes.

"What's wrong with you?" Naseema Madam asked.

"Nothing, nothing," Maryam Madam said, controlling herself. "Sometimes we forget who we're dealing with. How fast kids learn, how much they're watching us."

"I believe," I said hesitantly, "that a doctor can assert chastity. They would have to sign a certificate."

"You know everything, don't you?" Maryam Madam said, looking amused. "What do you think, Naseema? If she can produce a certificate of chastity, shall we sign one of these?"

"I can't be examined by a doctor without the permission of a guardian," I said, frowning. "So I can't produce the certificate of chastity unless I have that form first, to get a new guardian who can give that permission."

Naseema Madam clucked in disapproval and said, "It isn't right, to have so many hoops for us to jump through when we're just trying to do the right thing."

"What do you want to do about it?" Maryam Madam asked. "I said that we would make our decisions together, and I meant it. I won't go behind your back on this. The only thing I've learned in all these years is that when I find myself doing something alone, I'm usually doing something I shouldn't. We have a shared destiny, you and I, and the chance to either shape or destroy this girl's future."

She'd looked at me when she said it, so I knew she was trying to send me a message, meant for my mother. I remembered how relieving it had felt to share my pain with Mishail even for an instant. Why couldn't my mother do the same with Maryam? What use was it to hold my father's decisions against her? So what if they'd signed a marriage contract?

"We can't sign this document without proof of chastity," Naseema Madam said, and I made a sound of protest. She silenced me with a wave. "But that doesn't mean she can't have the document as it stands, which was how it was intended to be given. If she can find a way to prove her chastity and get the signatures to take to an *imam*, she can marry whomever she likes. Or maybe," she said with a look of contempt, "there are others who are less particular about that last detail of the law."

I saw a smile play on Maryam Madam's lips, as if she had succeeded in her true mission, the conversion of the black-and-white-thinking Naseema Madam to her own curvy Sudairi path. I wouldn't have been surprised if that wasn't her plan from the outset, breaking the Bilquis-like way of thinking in the straight lines of prison bars until—

I took advantage of both headmistresses looking at each other instead of at me and snatched not one but *all* the forms out of the folder, signed by the minister himself. If they noticed, if I was caught, I'd say it was an honest mistake.

—our minds were like the river, carving its route around and through even the hardest rocks of the earth.

22

SURAH AL-NISSA

Even ten-year-olds knew that the worst day in the year for a girl to be outside, curfew or no curfew, was Valentine's Day. Between police; Al-Hai'a; nervous brothers, fathers, and husbands; paranoid restaurant owners who preemptively closed up shop; and political protesters determined to make a point, the city had the volatility of gasoline.

Bilquis was right about one thing. It took a woman's mind to navigate the city's labyrinthine streets, to scheme some way of meeting up when under so much surveillance. *Muttaween* swarmed the Burger Kings and Herfy's in search of the potential indecency involved in Valentine's Day trysts. Police waited outside the men-only sections of Yamal

Asham and other hot favorites, trying to find women dressed as men. A poster from the hospital's psychiatric-care unit appeared on bus stops and taxi stands. *Be proud of your femininity*, it said. *The path of the* boyat *is not for you. In the* hadith *it is said, God is beautiful and loves beauty. Rise up against what confuses your feminine nature.*

So nobody expected us to be at Lenôtre restaurant, which on any ordinary day was packed with a wait list. It was far too romantic, far too *obvious*, and far too expensive. The four of us, Sofia, Aisha, Mishail, and I, arrived together in Mishail's car. I could see Aisha glaring at Mishail and knew what it meant. Had I not glared the same way at Daria for "stealing" Mishail? And where had that brought me?

It was time for us to adapt, to come up with a new plan, and I had the papers signed by the minister tucked into my skirt. I wasn't going to let them out of my possession for an instant.

I hadn't quite thought through what I was going to say, so we ordered food and talked about fashion and recipes, about how finals were coming up and how stressed out we all were about them. We were seated at the edge of the terrace, looking out at both the Faisaliyah and Kingdom towers. This was one of the few restaurants in the city where women were allowed to dine outside. I'd chosen it for a reason.

The *adhan* of the *isha* prayer rent the air and was

immediately followed by the citywide reverberation of shutters coming down in shops. Businesses were required to close for all five prayers, and in Riyadh, doors closed with a decided bang, and taciturn shopkeepers turned customers out the minute the *Allah-u-Akbar* sounded in the air. But our waiters made no move to stop service. Lenôtre was rumored to be one of the few places that allowed people to stay inside.

I was right. We were finally alone. While the prayer rang out, every *muttawa* in the city was either at prayer or rounding up miscreants from the streets and demanding they go to the nearest mosque.

"We don't have much time," I said urgently. "What I'm about to show you could change our lives forever. I need you to promise that even if you don't want to join me, you won't betray me."

"You don't need further proof from those of us in the *shillah*," Aisha said, tossing her head and including Sofia but not Mishail in her gaze. "You know that *we* at least don't run from the slightest inconvenience because we've lost our minds over a boy."

Mishail blushed but didn't say anything.

"*We*," I said, pointing to each of us in turn, "are the only *we* there is."

"We have to follow the rules if we want to include her in the *shillah*," Aisha muttered. "If she's willing to do that, I have no quarrel with her."

245

"What rules?" Mishail asked. When Aisha and Sofia looked away, she asked again, "What rules? I want to join."

"You have to share a secret that nobody else in this room knows," I said, "and give evidence of it into our safekeeping."

"We do what we can to help each other, and never knowingly harm each other," Sofia said.

"At least three of us," Aisha said, "which in your case means *all* of us, have to agree that you can be included."

"When you join us, you join us for life," I said, trying to gauge Mishail's expression. A part of me was nervous about including her. I may have misjudged the expression I'd seen on her face. We hadn't been able to talk freely in the last two days, and this wasn't the kind of thing you could discuss over the phone like a business meeting—*I think we're agreed, then, that we're both going to stop talking to Ahmed? That's what I read in your eyes, but I couldn't ask while the class was listening, so I thought I'd ask over the phone while your father might be listening. It's agreed, then?*

Mishail chuckled softly. Her eyes blazed with anger. She said, "It's sad, isn't it? That the only way to make a friendship last is to find ways to blackmail one another?"

Aisha looked ashamed but sulky, as if she recognized the truth of Mishail's words but didn't see any other way. I had to admit I didn't, either. Mishail was the equivalent of a human bomb. If she was on our side, she was a weapon to be reckoned with. But her influence and position made her a dangerous enemy.

"It's what I've wondered about in all the proposals that are coming for me," Mishail said. "What do they *really* want? The guy's the one who has to pay the *mahr*, so he's not exactly getting a bargain. Maybe he wants a friendship with my father, which is the oldest reason in the book to marry a woman. Maybe—and here I can dream—he's seen my eyes, or a photograph, or heard about me, and wants *me*, not the daughter of Minister Quraysh. And they're each willing to sign all kinds of things into the contract. One of them wants to give me a Cadillac I'll never get to drive. Another wants to buy me an apartment in Muscat for winter vacations. Once they've got me, though, I know how these things go. I'll be installed like a TV set in some apartment and told to occupy myself until I've had a child, while the guy moves on to the next thing. The next wife."

None of us said anything. I had assumed people would bang down the gates to marry Mishail, but I hadn't thought it had started.

"But here, I'll tell you the secret you're looking for. The one that you can use to destroy me, because I don't care if you do. I know what I have to answer for and to whom, and it isn't you, it isn't my father, and it isn't anyone in this world. I've decided to kill myself."

While we gaped in shock, the *adhan* sounded again behind us, a loud and long wail. We had only about thirty minutes before people would start coming in, sitting at the tables nearby for dinner. I felt a prickling at the edges of my scalp, as if the stubble of growing hair was shying away in horror.

"We're told that men are animals, that they can't control themselves," Mishail said. "That's why they whistle and holler at us at Faisaliyah. That's why we have to wear the *abaya*, because men can't be responsible for their behavior. So what do you make of it when the boy you love refuses to touch you? When he tells you that when you're married you'll take romantic vacations, he'll show you the world, he'll change society, but all the while you know he's in love with someone else? I sensed it," Mishail said, and her eyes locked with mine. "I always knew he wanted something else, but I kept believing he was just fighting his urges."

I swallowed, my face burning. Ahmed had made no promises to me about marriage. And except for that once, he had always touched me with restraint. I couldn't believe how far Mishail had gone, and I couldn't believe the casual calmness with which she was admitting to sin after sin. These weren't ordinary crimes, music tapes and jeans or dreams of tattoos and colored hair. Mishail had fallen into the kind of love we all ached for and yet feared, the obsessive and impossible hope we clung to that we would find a man who loved us enough to carry the weight of all our unanswered prayers.

"But all we did was talk. All night, all he wanted to do was talk. About my father. About how much he hated the ministry. He checked every wall and window for surveillance cameras, even when I told him they would never put cameras in a girl's bedroom. In the morning, he left without even saying good-bye. That's when I knew he didn't love me. He never had. He'd been using me to get information on my father. But that wasn't the worst of it. That isn't why I—" She swallowed. "He took a photo of me, a photo that I'd let him take as a token of my *love*, and he posted it online for his friends to comment on."

Aisha and Sofia looked between me and Mishail uncertainly, horrified mirrors of each other.

"And that wasn't the worst of it. The guys on the forum commenting on my looks, the girls commenting on my weight, everyone on the Internet having an opinion on how my eyebrows were shaped—I could have survived all that. The worst was when my father found out."

I gasped.

Mishail looked at me, her eyes full of love and gratitude, but also resignation.

"Yes, he saw it, before Leena took down the post. Nothing is ever really deleted once it's online. The ministry can always find it."

Mishail put her arms out on the table and rolled up her long sleeves to reveal deep bruises.

"He wasn't too happy," she said, laughing bitterly. "He moved me into my mother's room and made sure someone's with me at all times. The driver's out there, watching us, making sure I really am where I say I'm going to be. In two weeks he's going to marry me off to a colleague before I can damage his reputation even more. And then I'll be free."

"Mishy, you can't—"

"What do you want me to do, Leena? There isn't a single soul on earth I trust anymore. You always said you'd find a way, you'd never leave my side, and I trusted you to save me. So? Do you have a plan?"

I stared at her in stunned silence.

"Of course she does," Aisha said. "Leena always has an answer. So what's the plan?"

I showed them the papers I'd taken from Maryam Madam's office, told them in a quick whisper what they were, what I meant to do with them.

"Are you *joking*?" Aisha asked. "This isn't some high school prank."

"Good, because we graduate from high school in a month," I said. "You just heard Mishail. I'm not about to let her— Look, I'm going to do this. I'm only telling you in case you want to do it, too."

"I . . . would it work for Nasser?" Aisha asked. "He's in Dubai, and I'd heard—"

"It's the same form for marrying a non-Saudi as for marrying anyone else. It's an open slip, signed and ready whenever you are."

"But then we'd have to go to Dubai," Aisha said. "He

wouldn't be able to get a job here, but I can't travel without my father's permission. Oh my God, we're talking about jobs and marriage like we're grown-ups."

We grinned awkwardly, but Aisha was right. This was the first time we'd had conversations as women, about how we'd live out our lives. *Live* them out. We were making the biggest decisions we had ever made, all in the span of the *isha* prayer.

It was a good thing it was the longest prayer of the day.

"When?" Sofia asked.

"Next Tuesday," I said, looking at Mishail. Her face brightened as she understood. It was the day of the debate.

"The guy you're choosing," Sofia asked me slowly, "you're sure of him? I'm not sure I'd even trust my own brother with something like this."

"I'm sure. Mishail?" My heart was in my throat.

"If he consents," she said shakily.

"Are we really doing this, then?" Sofia asked nervously. "Once we do this, we can't go back. This isn't like choosing between college and working in a coffee shop. This is the rest of our lives. Can we really make a decision like this without—"

She broke off.

"Consulting our guardians?" I asked sarcastically. "That's exactly what I'm saying. That we're not going to be treated like children anymore. I'm tired of complaining about not having any choices. I'm tired of being helpless, waiting for some hopefully not awful guy to rescue me. So here's your freedom. Take it or don't, it doesn't matter, but for once, choose, and live with it."

Sofia stared at the table as the waiter brought us our check. Mishail paid it quietly.

"I guess if you're old enough to be married or taken to jail, you're old enough to choose your own husband," Sofia said. She shrugged and looked up. "I'm in."

Aisha said, "After this, we'll all be in our separate lives. How are we supposed to go on alone?"

"You're not alone," I said, kissing the top of her head as I got up. "The contract *you wrote* says we're in this together for life."

"You won't forget about me if I move to Dubai?"

"Aisha, darling, we can't do any of this without you. If your part doesn't work out, we'll all be packed off to jail. How are we supposed to forget the one who saves us all?"

Aisha burst into tears then, nervous laughter mixed with grief. In a few days we'd never see one another again, and I hugged her to hide my own tears.

On the way to the car, Mishail dragged me aside. Her eyes were wet, and she whispered, "You once asked why there weren't more of us out there. Do you see now what you can do that Manal couldn't? What *only* you can do?"

I shook my head. I told her it was chance, chance and the will of God, that I had been driven to such measures, that I'd taken law lessons, that I'd known to mention *adhl* to the minister at the right time, that I'd thought of this plan and taken all the forms and not just one for myself.

Mishail clicked her tongue in exasperation and nipped my ear fondly.

I grinned, because she only did that when she was truly happy.

23

INHIRAF

The days leading up to the debate were the most nerve-racking, slow days I'd ever experienced, and I was no stranger to the desert's heavy hours. You didn't need to watch the news to know that things were heating up again. Outside the malls, various posters cited phrases from the Quran, but no phrase was more prominently featured than the one at the center of the debate at the *Majlis—qawwam'una a'ala aln-nissa.*

Men are the guardians of women.

Outside Faisaliyah mall, the *muttaween*'s chants were growing more frantic. They now addressed women directly, yelling "Cover your eyes!" with increasing desperation, while women shot back with easy sarcasm, "Cover your own eyes, pervert. You're supposed to look away."

SUVs were always swarming around the major streets, Al-Hai'a waiting to catch women doing *something*. The minister appeared on television looking gaunt, as if he hadn't slept for a month.

"It is true that the Women's Council has submitted a recommendation that the *qawwama* of men over women be a recommendation and not a legal requirement," he said. "Even if it is ratified by the king, I urge caution and prudence in the application. The very fabric of society could be changed. This could plunge us into chaos."

Mishail used one of Rasha's burner phones that I'd given her to send me a message. *If this doesn't work, it's not your fault. At least you won't have to worry about my betraying you ever again.*

Don't be so dramatic, I sent back, my fingers trembling with fear. I knew it wasn't an idle threat anymore.

Over the weekend, in Mamlaka mall, a celebrating crowd of college students ended up fighting a bunch of the *multazimat*. The police could do nothing. It wasn't as if they could ask the women to leave the building and stand outside in the street without their guardians.

So when the minister announced a countrywide curfew that restricted women's movements after the *maghreb* prayer at sunset, I wasn't surprised at all. On TV, crazed-looking pundits asked what *qawwama* actually meant—protection? caretaking?—and what the issue was that meant stirring up a debate at the *Majlis*. What was wrong with wanting a man's protection from the dangers of life? A few concerned women, who were so concerned they were willing to appear on television, concurred gravely, stating that *qawwama* was a woman's right to a man's protection and that by making it a matter of choice, a life of abandonment and poverty could be forced upon half the country's population. How was a woman supposed to maintain herself without exposing herself to unspeakable dangers? There was at least one fatality on the roads of Riyadh every day. Were women supposed to drive in *that*?

Imam Fatullah said that the growing number of female preachers was an indication that women *wanted* guidance and stewardship and that only a few men (such as himself, of course) had stepped up to really reach the souls of women.

"A woman's deviant depths cannot be penetrated by ordinary words," he said with a knowing look, and for the first time since Ahmed had betrayed her, I heard Mishail laugh.

The word *deviant* made me uneasy, but not because I was insulted. It seemed to unlock a memory, one I couldn't place.

"We should play matchmaker," Sofia said, "and set Fatullah up with Bilquis."

"Don't even joke about that," Aisha said, glancing up from her collection of *hadith*.

A key turned in the door, and we stiffened and put on our veils. We knew from the exchanged glances and Aisha's nod that her father had come home and that he knew our plan. We were in her house, and at Dr. Haider's mercy.

If he helped us, we'd never be at the mercy of anyone else ever again.

If he gave us up, we'd never see the outside of our bedroom walls.

It caused me near physical pain to have to trust in the kindness of men this much. I swore that one day soon I'd have my own money in my own bank account, and I'd scrape camel dung all day if I had to as long as it meant I didn't have to beg for favors.

Dr. Haider walked in and rubbed at the checkered *shimagh* on his head as if he was exhausted.

"Whose bright idea was this anyway?" he asked. The others looked at me, and I raised my hand. "Do you even know what you're asking, girl? I don't even mean the certificates. If I wrote one without authorization, I could lose my license. But the test, the examination I have to perform before I can vouch for your chastity? It's terrible, and I'm not about to do it on three teenage girls whose guardians aren't even here."

The other girls shivered. None of us had really thought about what it would mean to prove our chastity. I had to admit I thought it would be a matter of testimony.

"Can't we just swear on it?" I asked helplessly.

"*Wallah*, you're such children!" he groaned. "Tahani, get in here!"

Aisha's mother walked in, looking unlike any woman

I'd ever seen. She was unveiled, of course, because the only men in her presence were her *mahrams*. But there was something truly stunning about her. There were edges of crow's-feet by her kind eyes, and dimples in her cheeks as if she'd spent so much of her life smiling that her face knew no other way to be. Her hair showed no signs of gray, and she relaxed against the doorway on one leg, as if she didn't have a care in the world.

I had never seen a woman look like that.

"Tahani-*habibti*," Dr. Haider said, almost shrinking in physical size to appear smaller than her, "do you know this grand plan that your daughter and her friends have cooked up?"

"Of course, dear," Tahani said, walking up to her husband and placing her hand on his thigh in perfectly comfortable affection. Aisha didn't seem to notice the insanity of it, but Mishail's and Sofia's raised eyebrows told me I wasn't alone in realizing that there was no couple we knew who doted on each other this much. It was unheard of.

"And you approve?" Aisha's father asked his wife. "That Aisha is to marry Nasser?"

"Much like his father, Nasser has never changed his mind once he's made a decision. The two of them want this, and our daughter brought it to our attention instead of slinking about in shame. I see no reason for these children not to experience the kind of happiness that Allah has shown fit to give us. Do you?"

"But the *tests*, Tahani!" Dr. Haider said. "The bloody tests!"

"Let me," Tahani cooed, and added, "Now go eat your dinner before you get even more grumpy."

Dr. Haider grumbled something under his breath but went off to the dining room. Tahani closed the door, and we unveiled.

"Aisha," Sofia said, "can I adopt your mother?"

Tahani laughed, a schoolgirl sound free of any worries. But she was no fool. She told us then all the secrets we would have to know, about mothers-in-law who searched the sheets after the wedding night for drops of blood, and why you couldn't store blood from your period to avoid suspicion. Thoroughly disgusted and terrified, we scowled at Aisha as if it were her fault we were here.

But Tahani kept rambling on with stories, adding at the end, "Not that any of you need to resort to the lamb's liver routine, you're all chaste."

"We could've told you that," I said, annoyed.

"Oh, sweetie, if you think this is disgusting, don't ever have children. They come out covered in blood and *everything*, and somehow you just don't care about any of it, you just want to hug the little things. I'm a nurse in the delivery room, you see."

We sat in silence, horrified by everything in general. Once we were veiled, Tahani went into the other room, and we heard her say, as casually as if she were passing her husband some more bread, "You can sign for all of them. It's written on their faces how little they know about anything. How's the lamb?"

Sofia was the first to break the tension.

"I changed my mind, Aisha. You can keep her. My mother's crazy, but even she doesn't go from talking about putting lamb's blood *inside* you down there to asking how the lamb you're eating tastes."

"Doctors are strange people," Aisha said. She had a faraway look. "So this is it, then. We're really doing this."

"I haven't got my part lined up yet," I admitted, dreading the conversations I needed to have. A part of me had put it off until we'd done this part, because I had thought it would be harder to procure certificates of chastity than it would be to find a man willing to marry me.

Faraz had technically not proposed, and what I was proposing was not just embarrassing, it was seven different kinds of perverse.

The quote I'd been struggling to remember popped into my head. *If we prevent Nature from reaching its object through a straight path, it would be forced to seek it through a deviant route.*

That was what my father had said that evening at the Quraysh house, while Mishail and I chased a helium balloon.

"Don't say such things in front of them," my mother had said.

"I wasn't talking about *al-inhiraf al-jinsi*," my father had replied, and this time all the other adults hushed him. That was when I'd started to pay attention. I remembered the words, understood them now thanks to Tahani's stories. *Sexual deviance.*

My father had laughed, an easy boyish laugh. "There are other, worse kinds of *inhiraf* that you can get forced into, isn't that right, *sadiq*?" He threw an arm around Mishail's father and drew him in close. "You may think you can play the game, twist yourself into the kind of person they want you to be without losing yourself. But the day will come when you'll have to choose, when you'll find your principles and your pride on one side, and everyone you ever loved on the other, and you'll have to close your eyes and jump toward one before you lose both."

I took in a deep, shuddering breath. When it came to the people I loved, I wasn't going to let my pride stand in the way. That was what my father had chosen, but I wasn't him.

I got up to leave, taking the *thobe* I'd packed into the bathroom. When I came out, dressed as a man, the girls gasped. They'd known I did this, but they'd never seen it.

"You look—"

"I know," I said. "Wish me luck."

It was a short walk to the Hosseins' house from Aisha's apartment. I knocked on the door and was shown in, given the usual automatic tea and sugar. I stirred it idly without drinking any.

"It's late for you to be here, isn't it?" Hossein asked,

coming out of his room and adjusting his *thobe*. He looked the same as he always had, an old man and a good one, steady in everything. For some reason, his measured gait touched me, made me feel warm inside.

"I've come to ask you for a favor, Uncle."

"There are no favors between us, child. Whatever you want is yours if I can give it."

I smiled.

"You've been everything to me. Teacher, father, employer. Can I really ask you for more?"

Hossein sat beside me on the sofa. He'd never done that before. He took my hands in his own freckled ones.

"You say these things because you're young," he said. "You don't understand, and you won't for a long time. A teacher's greatest happiness is a student's character. A father's greatest pride is a child's happiness. And an employer's greatest success is being able to support others. I've given you nothing that I didn't enjoy giving."

Tears pricked my eyes. I felt ashamed even for being here.

"Now there is one thing I wish you could give me," Hossein said. "But it has not so far been yours to give."

I looked up.

"Is it—" But instead of finishing my sentence, I showed him the two papers I clutched in the *thobe*'s wide pocket, the marriage license and a certificate of chastity.

Hossein coughed in surprise.

"How did you—"

"Water will find a way," I said.

Hossein examined both papers closely, holding the minister's signature up to his eyes for inspection.

"It's not a photocopy," I said.

"I can see that. I can see, but I don't believe. Our faith only trains us in the opposite, to believe what we can't see."

"Is this what you want?" I asked, clutching the sofa in a tight grip. "Faraz has never asked."

"Ah yes, I've told him not to," Hossein said, giving me back the papers. "I've wanted him to know the joy of love that is freely given, but as I said, it has not been yours to give."

"It is!" I cried. "It is, I swear."

Hossein looked at me, his eyes kind but knowing. He said, "If you loved Faraz, you'd have asked him. Women of our faith have always gone after what they wanted. Khadija chose her own husband, and Aisha bint Abubakr strode into battle on the back of a camel. But you came to me."

I put my face into my hands and sobbed. This conversation was not going at all as I'd expected. In a minute he'd tell me to drink some tea and go home, or worse, he'd drop me off himself out of obligation.

"The blessing of our time," Hossein said softly, "is the ease of acquiring a divorce. There are other places where a divorce is the same as a death sentence, but here . . . or in Morocco, for that matter, a divorce is easy and faultless. And if there are no children, finding another husband or wife is a matter of weeks. If a couple doesn't divorce within a year, that's how you know that what they have is real. Divorce is really a blessing for everyone, lawyers especially."

There was a twinkle in his eyes. I didn't understand. How could he make light of this? Was I going mad? But no, even Aisha's father had turned serious for a moment as I left, saying, "It's a good plan. I don't think they'll come after you. All their police and surveillance, they only look for people who break the law, not for those who use it to their advantage."

"When do you want to do this?" Hossein asked when my sobs quieted, and he looked at the papers again.

"Two days' time," I said, not understanding where he was going. He'd just been talking about the joys of getting divorced, but I wanted to get married.

"It can be arranged," he said. "There's still the matter of the *mahr*, but—"

"I don't care about *mahr*," I said, stung. "I'm not like that. And I don't plan on getting divorced!"

"*You* may not care about money," Hossein said absently, "but your father's a smart man. He knew people might try to steal you while he was away, and believe it or not they've tried. But your dowry is absurdly expensive. Why do you think your mother's been slaving away all this time?"

Realization struck. There was no way that night after

night of catering to Rashids, Rajhis, and Hariris was any-thing but lucrative. These were the billionaires who gave away diamond-studded watches as tips to waiters because they were two years out of fashion. My mother would have to be earning back not just her own dowry for a divorce, but enough to support a man who wished to marry me. With a sinking heart, I realized that even if we were now free to marry, men couldn't afford us.

"Isn't there a way for me to say I don't want a dowry? That I'll get a job?" I asked. How ridiculous, that the *mahr*, intended to protect us, was now the noose around our necks!

Hossein threw me a considering look. For a moment he switched from being the kindly old man I knew to being the sharp lawyer I respected and feared.

"You want something else, instead," he said, not a hint of doubt in his voice.

"Yes," I admitted, blushing. "I want to add a condition to the contract."

"That is your right, as the bride," Hossein said, and went to get a pen.

24

FITNA

There are certain days when you might feel wonderful until you step out into a gloomy, eerie fog, or other days when you feel as if the world is about to end but the birds are singing, and you might then wonder whether you've lost your mind, because you know there are no birds in the city of Riyadh.

My wedding was one of these surreal days. It was planned to happen at the same time as the debate. Dr. Haider had let us know through Aisha that if he was going to sign his name to something, he would see it through to the end, come what may. He would be there in person as a witness. Besides, he wasn't allowed to be at the *Majlis*, cheering his daughter on, so he would have to listen to the debate the way the rest of the country would. In the car, on the radio.

So while Daria and Aisha stepped out of the school bus, walking unsteadily up the steps of the Ministry of the Interior, I followed Aisha's gaze to the Lexus behind the bus. While the swarm of schoolgirls from across the country trickled in one direction to witness the first women's debate in the country, Sofia, Mishail, and I got quietly into Dr. Haider's car and were driven away to the registrar's office.

We traveled in silence, listening to the radio, to judges on the panel question various teams.

"More and more women these days, particularly those under Western influence, are declaring themselves to be atheists," said a judge. "Should we ban scientific education for women in favor of religious education?"

Aisha's response rang out, clear as a bell.

"The question you ask is a strange one, because there is no difference between religious and scientific education."

Pause for effect, I thought, and Aisha did.

A collective gasp hummed over the radio at the confidence of Aisha's words, at the way she spoke as if infused by the voices of angels. She said, "According to the *hadith* on cross-pollination in Medina, the prophet said we must seek knowledge even if we had to go all the way to China for it. That a man without intellect has no religion. And as the scholar Al-Ghazali said, if the soul has not been exercised in the sciences of fact and demonstration, it will mistake hallucinations for truth. A woman who avoids scientific knowledge out of embarrassment or fear is no *multazimat*. She is a heretic."

Dr. Haider laughed. "You did that," he said, looking at me. I was glad of the veil that kept him from seeing my face.

As with every other building in the country, we used the women's entrance to go to the marriage hall. Hossein had put our names down for an appointment, so the bored clerk simply told us what floor and room to go to. A large, mirrored wall separated the two women's elevators from the rest of the floor, giving the illusion of the four elevators that were actually there. It was strange to think of what might or might not be happening on the other side of the glass, in the parallel universe of men that controlled our little world.

Was Hossein waiting on the other side? What did Faraz think? He'd sent me a text message, his first and only message to me, the night after I'd spoken to his father.

I knew you'd find a way. :-)

That was all he said. No romantic overtures, no promises. Was I making a mistake? Was that why Hossein had run on so long about the ease of acquiring a divorce?

Sofia and Mishail held my hands on either side, but I felt cold and numb. My mind ran in circles, trying to think of alternatives, like a blind man in search of the fire exits.

My blood pumped so loudly I was certain it was about to burst out of my skin. My hands were sweaty, and I felt bad for having dragged Sofia and Mishail into this.

"Are you sure?" I asked them, my voice hoarse. "If you don't want to be here—"

Mishail just smiled and opened the door. Mishail's and Sofia's mothers were on the other side, standing with my mother.

My mother gave me an affectionate slap on the cheek and hugged me close, saying, "For a while there I was worried. I knew you were up to something; I didn't know what. If I'd known it was this . . . you wouldn't have had to be so alone."

I burst into tears, racked with nervousness. My mother hushed me, kissing my forehead and cheeks, telling me to be brave just a little longer.

"How long have you known?" I asked. "Did Hossein—"

"Maryam," my mother said. "Did you really think she wouldn't notice that all the forms were missing? She called me. We planned the rest. I called Hossein, told him to expect you. Here, hold on to these."

She pushed a small leather purse toward me, and I unzipped it to see passports and some other official documents inside, including an envelope filled with money. My eyes widened.

"I'm not leaving yet," I said. "School doesn't even finish

for *days*, and Faraz only begins at Qaraouine in August! And I can't leave the country without—"

"Your new guardian," she finished, her eyes shining. "I know. But you really think you can stay here after this? Don't worry, we've arranged everything. You can use the summer to get settled."

Her words finally made it real, and I started to shake as I realized I might not see her again for years. What would happen to her, to all the others who were helping us? What would happen when my father found out?

"Don't worry about us," my mother said, reading my anxiety. "They'll have to pretend they agreed to it to avoid the shame. They can't do anything else. You just have to get away before they find out."

The rest of the afternoon passed in waves of excitement and terror. When the *qazi* asked me if I agreed to the contract, I felt my throat move in slow motion, and I wondered if my voice would even work.

"*Khbal*," I muttered, losing almost all my vowels. Fortunately, Arabic didn't require them, and the *qazi* wrote down that I had accepted.

I was in a trance the whole time. When we were done, Sofia, my mother, and I were shepherded into Dr. Haider's car. Hossein, his wife, Faraz, and Mishail followed in another.

I received a text from Faraz.

Doesn't feel real, does it?

Do you regret it? I asked, heart pounding in fear. I hadn't been able to see his face yet, my *husband's* face.

Not for a second, he wrote back immediately, and I clutched the phone to my heart.

We drove past the *Majlis*, and I closed my eyes for a second and whispered a prayer for Aisha, that we might someday meet again.

We arrived at the airport and walked up to the counter. I hung back, knowing that this was the moment where everything could go wrong. For a moment I wondered how we could be held back from the open skies by nothing more than glass walls and red ropes.

"I can't believe you did this for us," Faraz said to my mother when she handed us our tickets. "I may have been accepted, but I couldn't afford to go."

She hugged him, whispered something that I was sure was the concentrated version of *take care of my daughter or I'll kill you*, given how he smiled at her. We were veiled fully as was required at the airport, so I couldn't see her face. It made my heart ache.

I'll come back for you, I promised her in my mind.

Faraz walked up to the desk and handed the tickets and passports to the official, who grumbled something over his shoulder.

"You think he suspects something?" I asked as I handed the marriage forms over. "The ink isn't even dry!"

"He was just saying that he's tired of all these summer

honeymooners," Faraz said. "The paperwork always lags behind, but there's no questioning the ministry's seal. Or the minister's own signature."

My mother's fingers found mine and clasped them tight. She was crying.

"I'm sorry," I said.

"Don't be silly," she said, rapping my knuckles. "What you're doing? Sacrifice like this, even the *thought* of it, it changes everything. It's what brought us together."

She glanced at the other women. Sofia's mother and Mishail's.

I frowned, not understanding what she meant. I wasn't sacrificing anything, unless she meant my enormously unaffordable dowry, which I'd chosen to concede out of common sense.

"Someday you'll see," she said, kissing my veiled cheeks fervently as Faraz approached us with our tickets.

"It's not over yet," he said. "The real trouble's the immigration on the other side. The law in Morocco forbids polygamy—"

"—except with the permission of the first wife," Hossein said gently, to calm us. "*Fi aman Allah*, children."

We walked past the red rope and into the waiting area. The ceilings of Riyadh airport were unnecessarily high, as if to make us feel our smallness. The chairs were uncomfortable, with hastily abandoned chewing gum stuck to the bottoms. We got in the airplane and took the four seats in the middle.

I closed my eyes, took a deep breath, and started muttering the first *surah* under my breath as the plane rumbled down the runway. I'd never been in an airplane, and I was terrified. The pit in my stomach grew and grew until it was nearly intolerable, and just when I thought I might start to cry, we were in the air. I was so shocked that we had actually come this far that I sat still and unmoving until the seat belt sign turned off.

There was a commotion as women got out of their seats and threw off their *abayas*. Men in *thobes* disappeared into the bathroom and returned in jeans.

Sofia ripped off her *abaya* as if it were on fire.

Mishail stared at her cell phone.

"Do you think the phone notifies him if I'm *above* the country?" she asked, taking out the battery and chip.

"Hey, Leena," Faraz whispered.

"Yes?" I said, surprised at the way my entire body shivered at his closeness.

"We're still within the national borders, and as you pointed out, the ink is not yet dry," he said, his lips brushing my cheek and making their way down to mine. "In case the plane gets turned around, there's something I've always wanted to do."

I laughed aloud and let our dreams take flight.

GLOSSARY

BOYAT   Tomboys, or girls who disguise themselves or act as boys

FAISALIYAH   A mall in Riyadh that has special zones for women

FITNA   Civil strife, loss of faith, or war within the Muslim world, a period of religious despair

GARAWIYYA   A naive, unpolished, or unmannered woman, for instance from a lower class or village

HARAAM   Forbidden

HIJRA The migration of the prophet from Mecca to Medina, the beginning of the Muslim calendar and Islamic history

HUZUN Despair and melancholy, spiritual anguish

INHIRAF Deviance

INSH'ALLAH If God wills

ITJIHAD A personal, intellectual, or spiritual struggle—searching one's soul for answers

KALAM EN-NAS Gossip, what people might say

KHULA Divorce initiated by the wife, as opposed to *talaaq*, which is divorce initiated by the husband

MULTAZIMAT Women committed to Islam

QAYAMAT Judgment or reckoning, the last day of the world, when God will separate the innocent from the guilty

RAMADAN Holy month, when one stays away from food and water from daybreak to sunset, and purifies the soul through prayer and avoidance of sinful thoughts

SHABAB   A group of young men

SHILLAH   A clique or small society

SHOUFA   The viewing of a bride before her marriage

SURAH AL-NISSA   The women's prayer, a verse in the Quran

TAAHUD   Confession signed by political activists that prevents them from blogging, speaking against the government, or leaving the country

TUFSHAN   Unharnessed bored or frustrated energy

UMMAH   Community (across geographies and time) of believers

WASTA   Influence or connections to power

WIRAN   Young, effeminate boy

WISKHA   Dirty, deviant, corrupt

ACKNOWLEDGMENTS

I would like to thank Julia Sooy and the crew at Godwin Books/Henry Holt Books for Young Readers for taking a chance on me. I am in awe over Aziza Iqbal's stunning cover art and Liz Dresner's design. Thank you to Laura Godwin, Melinda Ackell, Tom Nau, and the whole team at Macmillan for bringing this book into the world.

I owe so much to my agent, Kate McKean of the Howard Morhaim Literary Agency, for discovering the story buried in the sand and taking the time to make it shine.

I am grateful to Lydia Fakundiny of Cornell University, who taught me to write without fear, and to the poet Caroline Manring for teaching me to edit without mercy.

Finally, none of this would have been possible without my parents, whom I would like to thank for their absolute belief in me and their continued support of my atypical life.